I0692331

THE SILVER ALTAR

The Silver Altar

ROBERT ROSSI

ETERNEDITIONS™

New York

Copyright ©2023 Robert Rossi

Illustrations ©2023 Naomi Rosenblatt

All rights reserved. No part of this book may be reproduced or transmitted in any form or by any means, electronic or mechanical, including photocopying, recording or by an information storage or retrieval system now known or hereafter invented—except by a reviewer who may quote brief passages in a review to be printed in a magazine or newspaper—without permission in writing from the publisher.

Heliotrope Books LLC
heliotropebooks@gmail.com

ISBN: 978-1-956474-23-7
ISBN: 978-1-956474-24-4 eBook

For my wife Patricia,
the rock that supports me
in all aspects of my life.

CONTENTS

The Obelisk

THE OBELISK Major Characters

Father Leone: Prisoned Italian Army chaplain

Count Vittorio Farnese: Italian Army archeologist

Maria Luchese: Servant to the count

Marco Capitelli: Doctor of anthropology and archeology

Professor Guerci: Head of the University of Bologna's departments of anthropology and archeology

Chief Bordi: Bologna's security head

Father Mercogliano: Vatican security

Dottore Francesca Martini: Curator of Vatican Archives

Antonio Forte: Italian Minister of Economic Development

Assefa Berhane: Director of Ethiopian antiquities

Aamina Gebremichael: Assistant Director of Ethiopian antiquity

Carlo Monti: Undersecretary to Italy's ambassador to Ethiopia

THE OBELISK

Parma, Italy

Nestled in the Po Valley, astride the Apennines, Parma is a perfect basin for the northern Mediterranean moisture and the Alpine winds. Every autumn these two natural forces collide, creating a blanket of dense fog known as "La Nebbia," which envelopes the entire area. Besides altering the landscape, it has often altered the lives of those who live there.

PROLOGUE

1889
Axum, Ethiopia
Father Leone's Journal

March

From my cell, I hear the screams of my countrymen. Like me, they were captured and paraded before our African masters. The Ethiopians call our defeat the Battle of Adowa; Italy calls it our shame, and I call it our sin. We, the so-called bearers of civilization, were defeated by our arrogance and pride. Now, in my darkened cell deep beneath their ancient obelisk in their capital Axum, I await my death.

Emperor Menelik II decided to teach Italy and the Roman Church a lesson in humility. I, as the Italian Army chaplain, must write of our humiliation for the emperor so that Italians will never again consider invading their homeland. And our captors feel that the Roman Church would also share in this shame. My Lord, when will your creatures listen to you and not their pride? Italians will seek the sin of revenge, which will surely exceed the vengeance of my jailers.

May

My guards taunt me; they mock my faith in you. Grant me the strength to use my suffering for your glory. I pray that I can finish the task you have set for me.

Today another one of my comrades has died under unbearable torture. Tell me, Lord, how do I sing your praises when such evil triumphs? I must fight my demons of doubt.

July

I no longer hear the screams, now there is only moaning, yet I hear you, Lord. Will I have the strength to speak for you? Even now, in this abyss of hell, I feel your love and command.

Lift me with your spirit, your strength; I must write what you have impressed on my heart before I am too weak.

1935
Axum
Italian Invasion

The distant bombings from Il Duce's modern air force silhouetted the steep hills enveloping Abyssinia's ancient capital with a red tinge. Capitano Vittorio Farnese momentarily absorbed the image. He wondered how war could destroy, yet in some inexplicable way, create what seemed beautiful. But the stench of battle filled his nostrils, and any thoughts of beauty quickly evaporated. Glancing to his left he noticed the animated actions of his sergeant Pedone pointing to a precipice in a nearby cliff.

"What is it, sergeant?"

"Captain, we have found Italy's treasure!"

Italy's treasure, the captain thought, would be a term Mussolini would sell to the masses when it was a thinly disguised reason to steal the patrimony of another country. Rushing to the top of the cliff, Farnese saw a mammoth Obelisk piercing the red-soaked sky like a drawn sword.

Present Day
Parma, Palace of Colorno

Maria Luchese's ancient bones ached as if on schedule with La Nebbia. However, unlike the fog comfortably ensconced, her arthritis was anything but comfortable. Maria, in her seventies, had just marked five decades of service to the Farnese family. In her youth, she had been filled with longing and unspoken passion for her employer, Count Vittorio Farnese. His reputation as a daring archeological adventurer in Africa inflamed her nascent longings. But the desires of her youth had long cooled and were replaced by a loyal sense of duty to the count.

Making her way to Victorio Farnese's bedchamber in the former observatory room of the Colorno Palace, she thought of how many mornings she had brought the count a copy of *La República* along with his cappuccino. The count, now in his nineties, felt drawn to this room with its zodiac murals. He believed they lent some predictability to his long and eventful life. Knocking on the door, Maria waited for his reply.

When the count failed to respond, she slowly entered his room, calling out to him, *"Buon giorno!"* Then she saw an opening she had never seen before under the baroque fireplace mantle beneath the painting by Parmigianino. It appeared to be a dark crawl space. Could he be inside? Incredulous as that thought seemed to Maria, she called out, "Count Farnese?" She was greeted by silence. The idea of a man of his age and frailty being so adventurous as to explore this dark, suffocating space was incomprehensible. Peering into the darkened abyss, her gaze was met by the silent outline of the stilled body of the count clutching a blood-stained letter.

36 Hours Later
Bologna, Italy

"Wake up! Marco, wake up! Quickly!" Marco Capitelli's mother's voice disturbed his wine-soaked slumber—a slumber brought on by a long night of excessive drinking and song celebrating Bologna's triumph in soccer over Parma. Marco's own amateur soccer career and kicking skills helped to entice an extra drink or song. In Marco's opinion, Parma was a city of opera snobs who dared to believe their cuisine was superior to Bologna's.

As the room slowly came into focus, his mother, with her usual seriousness, repeated, "Get up, Marco! Professore Guerci is here in our house; he says it's urgent. What have you done now?"

"Maybe he understands what a special son you have."

Typically, Marco's humor missed its mark with his mother. Ten minutes later, in his parents' drawing room, the newly minted doctor of African anthropology and archeology, Marco Capitelli, met his visitor, the head of the university's department of anthropology and archeology.

Marco held out his hand. "How are you, *professore*? To what do I owe this honor?" Before he could respond, Marco continued, "Are you here to celebrate our triumph over the Parmiganni?"

"Marco, I don't share, how should I say it, your youthful exuberance. I hope you can see I'm here on a rather serious matter. A matter that involves someone you know, whose recent death has entangled our university with the interest of the State and the Vatican."

"Okay, *professore*, so we are not going to talk about soccer. I'm listening."

"Are you aware of the reported death of Count Farnese yesterday in Parma?"

Marco's well-practiced façade of cool detachment was pierced upon hearing this news.

The count was not just a teacher but also a mentor. Stunned into silence, Marco's head dropped, and he let out an audible sigh. He then resumed his cool demeanor and facing Professor Querci stated in a more somber tone: "No, as you may have guessed, I devoted myself to other matters yesterday."

Bologna
Carabinieri Headquarters

Marco entered the baroque chamber that served as the police interrogation room. He thought, *how Italian to beautify a room designed to elicit stress.* Present in the room with an air of command was Police Chief Ettore Bordi, easily recognizable from his many public appearances. The man standing to his left was Father Mercogliano, whom Professor Guerci whispered was the Vatican's security representative.

"Please sit, *signori.*" Police Chief Bordi gestured toward a bench beneath a painting of the Holy Family. Marco thought, *only Italy would juxtapose religion and the State in such a setting.* Not waiting to be introduced, Father Mercogliano focused his gaze on Marco while directing his statement to Professor Guerci.

"Professor, the Vatican feels that your protégé, Dottore Capitelli, has without sufficient scholarship embroiled the interests of the Vatican with the investigation of a suicide."

Looking at Chief Bordi for an explanation, the professor implored, "What is this inquiry about?"

"Count Vittorio Farnese's body was found less than forty-eight hours ago in his palazzo, apparently a victim of suicide," replied Chief Bordi. "Next to the body was penned a note stained by his blood. It stated, 'Marco, free my soul.'"

Leveling his gaze at Marco, the father said, "Dottore Capitelli, we know you and the count spent many days working on your thesis. Why would he make such a request about his soul? Are you, *Dottore,* with your new degree, able to free souls?"

Marco chose not to respond to his sarcasm but answered with a question. "By the tone of your questions, am I to assume that I'm a suspect in a suicide? It seems to me that it is a contradiction of *suicide* and *suspect.*"

"No, no, no, *Dottore,*" interjected Chief Bordi, "certainly not. We only want to examine your knowledge of the count in his final days."

"Well then, why does the Vatican profess such an interest in me?"

Impatient with Bordi's explanation, Father Mercogliano interjected, "The Vatican believes that your thesis about the theft of Ethiopian treasures lacks a true understanding of the church's role during those events. You, *Dottore*, seem to indicate the church's compliance with this theft. Your thesis, when placed under our scrutiny, shows little effort in searching our archival resources. Your unorthodox viewpoint has reached the Ethiopian authorities. I'm sure you're aware that after seventy years, Italy has returned the contested obelisk to Axum. The suggestion of Vatican complicity has, to use an American expression, 'opened up a can of worms.'

"The Ethiopians are questioning the church's motives. They now believe we not only absconded with their heritage, but we have knowledge of their patrimony that we are not sharing with them. Your thesis references a 'Latin rite' inscription that appears in an area beneath the obelisk. According to your thesis, Count Farnese received illumination from this inscription."

Chief Bordi interjected at this point, saying, "The Ethiopian embassy in Rome believes that the interest of the Vatican and the State seem to be in collusion. Therefore, your term *Latin rite* suggests Italian knowledge and advantage over their State during a sensitive period in their history."

Bordi further noted that after the return of the obelisk in 2005, new and potential economic partnerships with Ethiopia were now tenuous. "Can you expound on the correlation between your use of the term *Latin rite* and the count's illumination?"

1937
Axum, Ethiopia

Captain Vittorio Farnese moved slowly behind the crane, positioning himself alongside the obelisk of Ethiopia's Emperor Melanik the First. Mussolini's orders were to bring his "prize" to Rome without delay. The captain's need to respect this historical site and its archeological importance outweighed his orders. Farnese determined to delay this project just long enough to explore the chambers below the obelisk and catalog the findings for posterity. Citing a lack of proper military procedure, Farnese barked orders to the crane crew to cease and desist. He knew this would buy him a few weeks, considering the Italian Army's well-founded reputation for inefficiency.

Entering the radial corridor beneath the base of the obelisk, and descending a narrow shaft into darkness, Farnese and Lieutenant Corti, a fellow archeological enthusiast, set out into the gloom. Straining with the feeble light barely illuminating rock-cut chambers, they passed the tombs of Ethiopia's royalty. Behind them the clear Axum sky no longer permitted any light. Unique Abyssinian murals depicting the lives of Ethiopia's kings were barely visible. The interior was cool and damp, with three parallel rows of columns and chambers on either side. Here were carved reliefs and statues of New and Old Testament figures. In the center, a stone table and golden cross. Above, in still luminous colors, was a mural depicting the story of the birth of King Melanik the First, the product of the union of King Solomon and the Queen of Sheba. Ethiopians, like the ancient Egyptians, prayed for their royal dead.

While cataloging, Farnese and his lieutenant spotted something unexpected, a steep and narrowing descent, in the east chamber. They wondered if what they saw in the pale light was an illusion. With their lamps weakening and their growing sense of disorientation, they saw life-sized murals depicting what appeared to be angels. A startled Lieutenant Corti touched the captain's shoulder while motioning his head toward the wall to their right. There, mural figures of the archangels Michael and Raphael were posed with their backs turned to the viewer, their swords crossed. Raising their lamps to the inscription beneath the mural, Farnese read out loud the Latin rite, "God's Raft on Rome."

Present Day
Bologna
Carabinieri Headquarters

Marco considered his use of the term *Latin rite*. Finally, after a few moments' reflection, he explained, "The count believed he and his lieutenant stumbled upon some anomaly, while excavating the Melanik obelisk in Axum. In our conversations he hesitated in expounding on the meaning of the anomaly, and when pressed by my inquiry he deflected the line of questioning with the word *illumination*. To my mind the term *Latin rite* suggests some script, possibly carved.

"As to his point of 'saving his soul,' anyone who knows me knows that gift is well out of my providence. Some say my talent lies in leading souls in the opposite direction."

Father Mercogliano, visibly agitated by Marco's apparent flippancy, snapped, "Dottore Capitelli, are we to believe that the count would withhold information about such a discovery? His whole career was one of firsts; why not let you in on another of his discoveries?"

"Father," Marco replied, "the count was extremely generous with his time on my behalf. There is no reason that I can fathom why he would withhold information about this discovery. Perhaps, he felt a man of his stature did not need to announce a discovery."

"Dottore, surely the count with his access to the powers that be at the Vatican, knew of the political ramifications with Ethiopia."

Professore Querci, visibly agitated, interrupted. "Gentlemen, I can assure you that Dottore Capitelli and I were never given information that would compromise the State or the church. I reviewed Marco's thesis every step of the way. It would have occurred to me if we violated ours or anybody else's authority."

Inspector Bordi and Father Mercogliano conferred for a moment. Then turning to the others, Bordi said, "We have concluded that although you are innocent of withholding information, you can and should lend your service to alleviate the current strains in our relationship with Ethiopia. We, the State and the church, would like Dottore Capitelli to accompany our respective representatives on a fact-finding search for the true meaning of the count's discovery."

Marco's cynicism surfaced immediately. "Does this mean a whitewash of the inconvenient truth to preserve diplomatic relations—or should I say economic well-being?"

Father Mercogliano quickly rejoined. "Let us hope that your conceit doesn't blind you to your duty to the church."

Reflecting a moment and realizing the pressure brought to bear, Marco quietly acquiesced. "When and where do I begin?"

Two Weeks Later
Rome, Da Vinci Airport

Marco's anticipation of meeting his government and Vatican travel companions conjured multiple emotions that ranged from unwarranted intrusion to mild curiosity. His gaze rested upon an attractive twenty-something blonde with piecing almond-shaped eyes and just a hint of green behind those alluring long dark eyelashes. Her tailored, form-hugging beige suit revealed a hint of the knee to trigger his inner libido. An officious middle-aged man accompanied her, thin and well turned out in an Armani suit. Within moments he heard her mention his name and saw their hands were extended to greet him.

"Dottore Capitelli, I am Francesca Martini, curator of the Vatican archives, and this is Antonio Forte of the Ministry of Economic Development. Your gaze seems a bit perplexed, *Dottore*; why?"

"Pardon my expression, Signora Martini," Marco replied. "I didn't expect the Vatican to send such a young person on a complex mission."

"I could say the same about your relative youth," she responded. "But I believe you didn't expect to see a woman in my position. I would have assumed that someone of your generation would not be so sexist."

This is not going so well, Marco thought. Signore Forte motioned to his companions that the boarding sign for their flight from Rome to Addis Ababa had just been posted.

Marco found the flight uneventful, and his traveling companions appeared more remote than Ethiopia. His attempts to engage in conversation with Francesca were met with cool detachment. Wanting to revise her first impression of him and motivated by her beauty, Marco asked her if he could explain his initial comments upon meeting her.

"*Dottore*," she responded, "I'm sure your callous remarks when we met were consistent with your reputation."

"I've been insulted many times, Signora, but never so eloquently. I'm sorry to see you so resolute on this matter, particularly given that we must work so closely together in the coming days. At least let me attempt to change any impressions you have formed."

"*Dottore!*"

"Please call me Marco."

"*Va bene*, Marco. You obtained a position and title from a prestigious university in a serious field. A respected professor taught you, and you were mentored by one of Italy's most famous archeologists. Although your scholarship is impressive, your callous comments about the people and authorities that formed your success indicate an immature and self-centered individual."

Visibly stunned and mustering his remaining pride, Marco responded, "Francesca, whether we like it or not, we will have to work together."

"Yes, Marco, like you say, 'whether we like it or not.'"

Addis Ababa
International Airport

The flight was uneventful, if not painfully quiet, given Signora Martini's self-imposed silence. True to Marco's expectation, Addis Ababa was sundrenched, but the city's bustling populace challenged his perception of the slow-paced Sub-Saharan capital.

Spotting their Ethiopian counterparts, Antonio Forte waved and shouted, "Assefa!"

Turning to his travel companions, he said, "Assefa Berhane is an old friend; her name means birth light." Then, turning to Berhane, he said, "I'm honored, my old friend, to have you meet my companions."

Ms. Berhane introduced them to her associate, Ms. Aamina Gebremichael, her country's director of antiquities. Marco observed her classic Ethiopian features, golden brown skin with a wide brow and beautiful dark eyes. She and Ms. Berhane exhibited physical grace, a trait that he considered common among Ethiopians.

Ms. Berhane announced, "Tonight, you'll rest. There will be plenty of time for business tomorrow."

"Am I correct, Ms. Gebremichael, that it is the custom in your country to take the father's name and give that name as the surname to the children, hence your name Michael?"

"Yes, Signore Capitelli, you are correct in your cultural awareness. I hope you will exhibit further sensitivity to our customs as we try to alleviate our respective suspicions."

Respective suspicions are no doubt a not-so-veiled reminder of Ethiopia's reluctance to forget Italy's 1935 invasion of their proud country. Italians of Marco's generation, like what Americans call millennials, tend to view history before their birthdate as ancient. Well, maybe not so ancient in Marco's case since his chosen profession is steeped in history.

Next Morning
Lobby of the Addis Ababa Hilton

As the Italians finished their first enjoyable foray into the pleasures of Ethiopian coffee, Antonio remarked, "As you know, our government has an uneasy political and economic relationship with this uniquely beautiful country. Let us go over some salient points before we meet our Ethiopian hosts. Francesca, could you inform us about the church's difficulties with the religious authorities after I'm through?

"It is important to remember that since the overthrow of Emperor Haile Selassie in 1974, Ethiopians have experienced famine, war, and failed Marxist utopian economic and social engineering. Despite thirty-five years of near economic collapse, the country remains wedded to one-party rule. They still discourage private investment and show a marked preference for state control. China, which in many ways shares values and does not concern itself with this country's human rights violations, has been given the green light to build roads to access remote regions. Italy, however, has been frozen out of potentially lucrative projects such as the Renaissance Dam, owing to our turbulent past with them. Hold on a minute. I see Carlo Monti, the undersecretary to our ambassador to Ethiopia, arriving." Rising and extending his hand to the official, Antonio said: "Signor Monti, you have arrived just in time to brief us on the existing political climate."

"Thank you, Signor Forte," Carlo Monti replied. "As you know from our history, Italy in 1889 had the distinction of being the only European power to be defeated by an African nation. This remains a great source of pride for this proud country. General Oreste Baratieri became a symbol of Italian shame, and Emperor Menelik the second the symbol of Ethiopian pride. Normally, when a nation defeats another, the victor can afford to be magnanimous. However, Italy did not recover from that 'shame' until forty-six years later. Tragically, the successful 1935 Italian invasion and its subsequent pillaging of their national treasures removed any vestige of rapprochement. All one must do is realize that it took seventy years for their government to get back the obelisk, which is rightfully theirs. You can imagine the sensitive minefields we face in our current assignment. I will talk more on this subject in the ensuing days. Seeing that we have little time, I would like to ask Signora Martini to address the delicate state of Vatican and Coptic relations."

"Thank you, Signore Monti," said Francesca Martini. "It is important for us to remember that before the incursion of Islam along the Horn of Africa and modern-day Sudan, the church of ancient Ethiopia was in communion with Rome in the West and Constantinople in the east. However, long centuries of separation lead to the development of the Coptic Church we witness today. The belief that Menelik the First, the son of King Solomon and the Queen of Sheba, brought the Ark of the Covenant to this land, helps explain the rich Jewish connection running through Coptic religious practices. Until the recent return of the obelisk, the Vatican was not allowed to have open diplomatic relations with the Ethiopian government. Consequently, the papal legate for our church was appointed out of Cairo, not Rome. Only now, following the return of the obelisk, have the Coptic and Ethiopian authorities accepted a direct representative from the Vatican. Still, we are not allowed to proselytize. The old habit of viewing the Roman Church as an arm of the Italian government dies hard."

Looking at Marco somewhat disdainfully, she said, "Of course, it's understood that we must exhibit sensitivity and patience when proceeding with our assignment. I see our host arriving. More on this later."

Francesca's disdainful glance disrupted Marco's joy in listening to the historical references to a part of the world that had more than its fair share of mystery, both historical and religious.

He resolved to change that misfortunate first impression she had of him. Marco didn't believe his charm with the opposite sex was no longer effective. Certainly, an Italian athletic, handsome man in his twenties could not fathom such a catastrophe.

Later That Day
Enroute to Axum

Passing through the town of Lalibela on their way to Axum, Marco felt the urge to show his appreciation for Ethiopia's architectural heritage. Commenting on the unique beauty of their rock-hewn, cross-shaped churches, he stated, "Ms. Gebremichael, one of the reasons I specialized in Ethiopian archeology is because I am fascinated with the unique carvings of your churches in solid rock."

"Signore Capitelli, you know, of course, about the legend of how it was carved?"

"Well, I know it had some divine intervention."

"More precisely," noted Ms. Gebremichael, "King Lalibela would carve one meter during the day and during the night, angels would carve three meters. We Ethiopians, unlike most of our African neighbors, use our religious myths to bind our sense of nationalism. This accounts for the numerous pilgrimages to these historical sites. Our history has remained untainted by European influences, save for your Italian intrusion." She looked directly at Marco, noticing his flinching facial demeanor. "Consequently, our religious practices have remained pure, unlike other African countries."

Marco noted the inflection of distrust in her tone; he did not doubt that they would face difficult moments in their quest for detente in the ensuing days.

In the Ethiopian highlands, Axum presents itself as a naturally fertile, beautiful, and defensible area. The Ethiopian hosts took great pleasure in elaborating on the lives of the notable kings and queens who reigned in this storied capital. The Italians were given an overview of Axum's repertoire of treasures, most notably the Church of Saint Mary of Zion, which was reputed to house the Ark of the Covenant.

The many obelisks, some seventy meters high, that punctuate the skies were even more majestic than Marco had imagined.

"That is the 'tomb of the false door,'" exclaimed Assefa Berhane. "The ancients made their tombs and obelisks in the form of houses where the spirits could dwell."

Marco noticed the delegation's immediate attention was focused on the fallen obelisk looming ahead.

"That broken object is the obelisk you returned to us after seventy years," intoned Aamina Gebremichael. "Do you not agree that we should receive some help in restoring it to its former glory?"

Her question was met with silence. Marco thought the broken obelisk a fitting metaphor for the state of Italian and Ethiopian relations.

Entrance to King Menelik's Tomb

Marco's belief that the task ahead would be a quiet affair was dashed when the Italians saw the extensive crowds gathered at the obelisk.

Francesca whispered to Marco, "You can see that our task will be extremely delicate. Any perceived slight to their national pride could have unpleasant political consequences."

"Signore Monti," inquired Aamina Gebremichael, "Are you and your team aware of the journal of Father Leone?"

"Yes, we are," interjected Francesca. "We know your country has used his words to justify Ethiopia's claim to have fought a just war against Italian aggression in 1889."

"Do you think his words were forced?" Ms. Gebremichael asked.

"Certainly not. A priest is duty bound to speak the truth."

"Then let us prepare to enter this tomb."

Although Marco, through his research, had seen many images of the tomb, none prepared him for the stark environs of the cavernous site and the shifting shadows that enveloped the stone figures. A perceptible drop in temperature gave note to a feeling of dread.

"Signore Capitelli." Ms. Gebremichael lowered her voice to reflect the sacredness of the space. "The tomb lighting will serve our team for only the most trafficked or tourist-treaded pathways. Concerning our purposes, we will soon have to rely on our portable power sources."

"I suppose the tomb has been completely explored," noted Francesca.

"We don't have the resources of your country to *fully* explore, so let us hope that Italy's renowned team will find this elusive 'Latin rite' script."

The elongated dark pathways and lack of conversation on the part of their Ethiopian hosts punctuated the Italian team's innate sense that the Ethiopians resented their presence.

Suddenly, Marco felt a perceptible angle of descent in the passageway. This change triggered in him a memory of his mentor Count Farnese. Marco recalled a conversation where the count described a similar descent.

"Marco, this exploration changed me, and this tomb, as dark as it seemed, enlightened my soul." These words, with oblique spiritual references, filled Marco's thoughts. Why did the count, not known for his religiosity, use such a term? It was rumored that the count's former fascist affiliations would not encourage such spiritual references in their verbal bantering.

Returning from his musings, Marco turned to his associate. "Remember, Francesca; we are looking for either a carving or a mural of archangels. They could be any place, most likely in the area used to keep the Italian prisoners. The count knew of Father Leone's diary."

"Yes, Marco, this we already know. I'd hope you could offer more before we lose the tenuous patience of our Ethiopian hosts."

"Francesca, the count referred to a discovery that he kept to himself. This suggests he found something that enlightened him, but he didn't share it with the State or the church. Almost certainly the Ethiopians are as much in the dark about this as we are."

"Be that as it may," Francesca intoned. "It's not substantial enough to resolve our dilemma, namely, finding this Latin rite." Of course, Francesca's remark was correct. However, Marco was hoping for a bit more comradery instead of her steely sounding professionalism.

"Always view Ethiopian tombs through the prism of the Old Testament," Marco remembered the count's words.

Just then, the explorers felt a perceptible decline in their descent, with a noticeable shift to the left.

"Marco, why do you hesitate?"

"Francesca, Count Farnese said 'to see this tomb as if you were a Levite priest.' What is it about Jewish burial rites that might give us a clue? Signora Martini, can you tap into your ecclesiastical knowledge and help?"

"Well, offhand, I'd say tombs were carved facing Jerusalem, and prisoners would defile a sacred area," replied Francesca.

"Francesca, you may have just cracked the code. We need to move to the right where the passageway descends away from any sacred area." Recalling the words of Father Leone's journal that referenced Italy's shame, Marco stated, "In the Jewish Bible, angels were used to separate the good from the bad."

"So, Marco, are we now looking for angels?"

"We are looking for prisoners kept away from the sacred areas of this tomb. Now we were told that the Ethiopians have not fully explored the tomb, correct?"

"Your point being?"

"Francesca, most Christian churches in these locales were built over ancient sites of pagan worship. Count Farnese knew of pre-Christian and pre-Judaic elements in this tomb."

"I fail to see your point, Marco; how would this help us?"

"There has to be a lower chamber, a pre-monotheistic chamber."

"Are you saying that the Italian prisoners, particularly Father Leone, were buried there?"

Without replying, he turned to their Ethiopian guides and asked if there was a historical lower chamber in the opposite direction of the current Christian one. Ms. Berhane and Ms. Gebremichael nodded in unison, immediately pointing to a statue of St. Michael with his foot firmly planted on Satan's head.

Francesca reminded Marco that St. Michael was often used as God's warrior to suppress evil.

"May we explore this sacred area?" Francesca implored.

Marco quickly realized the value of Francesca's quiet professional demeanor and its beneficial effect on their Ethiopian hosts. He also realized she might suspect that the Italian prisoners may have been ensconced there.

After a brief consultation with Ms. Gebremichael, Mr. Berhane asked if the Italians knew what lay beneath. Marco said he knew Italian prisoners were detained in an area beneath the obelisk that would not defile any of the Ethiopian sacred places of worship.

"Your respect of our holy places does you credit; you may proceed," replied Berhane.

Francesca asked, "Can we get help to move the statue?"

"We will get you the necessary labor," replied Ms. Gebremichael.

Later
Exploring the Sacred Space

Peering into a dark abyss, their nostrils were immediately filled with an odor of decay. The Italians and Ethiopians descended slowly down stone steps not used in 123 years. Marco probed the surrounding walls looking for any indication of a jail cell or closed door.

"Beelzebub!" screamed Francesca.

"What did you say?" Marco asked.

"Beelzebub, look over to your right—*Beelzebub, the devil.*"

"Well, actually, Ms. Martini, that's the Ethiopian pre-Christian god of the underworld; I guess it's our forerunner of Lucifer," replied Ms. Gebremichael.

Marco suddenly remembered Count Farnese's saying that he and Lieutenant Corti *passed through Hades and paid the ferryman,* an obvious reference to old Beelzebub.

The area near the ancient statue carried the stench of blood with a stillness punctuated by a wisp of air. Standing still and asking his party to listen intensely, Marco strained to hear something he thought was in motion.

"What is it, Marco? What do you expect to hear down here, Father Leone's cry for help?"

"Francesca, I appreciate the levity, but I think I heard running water. Is there a river source above ground?" Marco asked his hosts. "If yes, is there an ancient riverbed down at this depth?"

"Well, as a matter of fact, yes. Over the millenniums the river shifted and silted. What you hear is a residue of the current river."

"Fine. Lead me in the direction of the moving water."

"Why, Marco? Why the water?" Francesca asked.

"The count once said that in pre-Coptic culture, if you separated evil from running water, evil could not cross the divide. What does that suggest to you, Francesca?"

"Well, maybe Italian prisoners were held nearby. Let's go; the air is beginning to stifle my breathing." Francesca motioned to the Ethiopians, pointing toward the perceived sounds.

Passing the demonic statue with its eyes now given to corrosion and rodent feces, the explorers felt moisture enveloping their movements. Ahead appeared a pool of water, not quite a running river, more like a dank pond. Yet, the faint sound of moving water was sensed. On the wall behind the pond was a dim outline of painted figures.

"Ms. Berhane, please aim your light at these figures."

Astonishingly, a life-sized mural of two angels appeared with their backs turned to the viewers.

Francesca noticed a slight smile appear on Marco's face. "Why the smile?"

"If I'm not mistaken, we may have arrived at our destination."

"How so?"

"Count Farnese once told me that angels were used to either block an entrance—think of the Garden of Eden—or keep evil at bay—think of St. Michael slaying the dragon. If the evil is hemmed in, the angels face the evil; thus, their backs are turned to us."

"Ms. Gebremichael, can you date the mural?" asked Francesca.

"Off hand, without total certainty, I'd say it's the style of one hundred and fifty years ago."

"Francesca, look carefully. The 'Latin rite' should be nearby. One hundred and fifty years dovetails with Father Leone's timeframe."

Shining their light sources over the angel murals, an inscription in Latin appeared carved into the stone.

As Marco began translating, Francesca interrupted him and quickly stated, "'*God's Raft on Rome.*' His cell must be here, but where? There are no doors or obvious portals."

"Francesca, look at the pool of water. What is it that appears incongruous to you?"

"It looks like clear water."

"Exactly, it's clear. It suggests movement; does it not?"

"Yes, yes, the water is moving ever so slightly toward the wall with the inverted angels."

"Ms. Berhane, can we measure the depth of this pond?"

"Yes, Signore Capitelli. I'll place this light on the surface of the water. That might indicate its depth."

Moments later, Berhane responded, "It appears that it is no more than four and a half to five feet, and the floor is solid stone."

Marco slowly descended into the pool; taking a deep breath, he submerged beneath the surface. Aiming his flashlight, he saw the wall with the mural left an opening of three feet. At that moment Count Farnese's words, *"I found myself crawling in a dark tunnel of water,"* sprang to his mind. Rising quickly to regain his breath, he turned to Francesca and asked if she could tie a rope to him.

"Why Marco, why the rope?"

"If I'm right, Father Leone's prison cell can be reached by crawling under the wall that seems only about a foot in width. The rope will allow me to signal to you that I found it and it's breathable."

Descending with the fastened rope, Marco swam through the narrow passageway and emerged on the other side into what appeared to be a chamber with an elevated stone floor above the water line. He raised himself onto the dry platform. Setting up his lighting equipment, he was stunned to see a metal crucifix clutched in the hand of human skeletal remains. A skeleton still in its tattered Italian chaplain uniform. A chamber pot and a few corroded wooden utensils were all that survived in this dank and humid cell. From the hollowed eyes emerged a small rodent. The thought occurred to Marco that they must have feasted on the remains of this poor soul. He dismissed the thought as too gruesome to dwell upon, particularly that they might not have waited for the victim's passing.

It seemed that this must be Father Leone, but how to be sure? As Marco backed up, he hit the wall behind him. As he quickly turned around, the answer became clear.

Minutes later, and joined by the explorers in the hidden cell, Francesca's eye's widened with astonishment as she began to read the scratched carvings on the wall.

"Marco, do you see what this means?" she asked.

"Yes, he is atoning for the Italian invasion. He offers his life to 'our Lord.' It's clear what we need to do."

Turning to their Ethiopian guides, the Italians explained their revelation. Mr. Berhane agreed that the task for both countries was to bring the light of revelation to their respective authorities.

Rome
The Vatican
Press Conference

"Are you ready, Marco? We're getting the signal—you're on next."

"I'm about as ready as I'll ever be, Francesca. These Vatican murals and significant notable religious clerics have an unsettling effect on this simple Bologna boy."

"I doubt that, Marco. Simple is not a word I would associate with you; besides, I think you are about to get your cue."

Approaching the dais with cameras flashing, Marco noticed Professor Querci.

Smiling, the professor gave him a nod of encouragement. Drawing a big breath, Marco began to speak.

"I thank you for this opportunity to address the representatives of our respective governments, especially here in the halls of the Vatican. Much of what I am about to say befits this setting. Count Vittorio Farnese, as some of you may not know, was my mentor. He was, as many of you know, a lauded Italian adventurer.

"When I was initially approached to undertake the task of *'Marco, save my soul'*—which were the count's last words—the request felt daunting. It wasn't long before this request by my government and the Vatican to help alleviate tension between Ethiopia and Italy overwhelmed any sense of confidence my youthful bravado tried to demonstrate.

"One hundred twenty-five years have passed since the first Italian invasion of Ethiopia. Our respective nations may finally experience healing from the damage of two wars, occupation and theft. I hope that what I relate to you today will help heal my mentor's request. I don't presume to say with certainty that I will succeed.

"Our Ethiopian hosts, ably represented here today by Ms. Gebremichael and Ms. Berhane, impressed our exploration party their national sensitivity to any incursion into their sacred places. The details of our exploration are in the handouts distributed to you earlier. Suffice it to say we located the tomb, or rather I should say prison, of Father Leone. Father Leone's journal is well known in Ethiopia as an apology for the 1889 Italian invasion. Count Farnese discovered his prison cell, yet never reported it to his fascist superiors. The triumphant return to Rome with Ethiopia's obelisk in hand and Mussolini's acclimation to glory combined to silence the count's conscience. Yet that conscience surfaced throughout his life. Often, in moments of reflection, the count would indicate oblique remorse. This remorse was never defined; certainly my twenty-something, self-absorbed nature neglected to inquire further.

"The count had discovered that Father Leone carved in his cell words meant to offer his life in atonement for the invasion. Obviously, Mussolini and his minions would never agree to let this tarnish any sense of fascist glory.

"I believe the count wanted me to bring this to light; I also believe that our church needs to know that Father Leone followed Christ's call for sacrifice to the fullest measure. Our Ethiopian hosts tell me that the measure of the father's sacrifice has helped to heal the rift between our nations.

"Let us remember that these two men lived and died as patriots to their faith, not just their nation. Thank you."

Francesca approached Marco, touching his elbow as he stepped off the dais.

"I want to say, Marco," she whispered, "that I may have been unfair in my original characterization of you. I've come to see your qualities of compassion for others."

"Oh, Francesca, you were right the first time; don't have me canonized. It's not good for my bad boy image."

"Be that as it may, Marco. Can we be friends?"

"Sure, Francesca. Actually, I was hoping you would be my dinner companion tonight. I'm told the Hotel Eden's roof has a breathtaking view of Rome."

"I'd love to join you, Marco."

"You know, I never asked, where do you come from?"

"Oh well, with my expertise in food and the opera—that could only mean Parma."

God, he thought, *another Parma snob; just my luck.*

The Silver Altar

THE SILVER ALTAR Major Characters

Marco Capitelli: Italian archeologist

Francesca Martini: Senior Vatican archivist

Lieutenant Patricia Conway: Annapolis naval historian

Captain Mark Rossi: Head of Annapolis historical research department

Second Lieutenant Orbani: Annapolis linguistic expert

Doctor Benedetto: Chief Vatican historian

Father Omar Hassen: Coptic historian and Vatican liaison

Geena Chiesa: Concierge in Rome

Thomas Colt: Security chief at the American embassy in Sudan

Mohamed Sallah: Sudanese security chief

Omar Kahib: Former Sudanese security chief

Alessio Monti: Italian chemist and friend of Marco Capitelli

THE SILVER ALTAR

AD 632: The prophet Mohammed declared from his death bed to his followers: "Rome shall fall!"
With tears and swords raised, they swore: "Rome shall fall!"

AD 800: Kneeling before the Roman Pontiff, the Frankish king Charlemagne, at six feet six inches, still appeared equal in stature to the diminutive Pope Leo. He is crowned Holy Roman Emperor in Rome's Basilica of St. Peter.

AD 809: In gratitude, Charlemagne bestows a Silver Altar forged by artisans steeped in the skills of classical Roman sculpture and personally selected from Rome's eastern empire expressly for the Basilica of St. Peter.

AD 846: Islamic pirates sail up the Tiber and attack Rome.

"The Roman wall is holding effendi. Our battle ramps are useless. Pray that Allah will show us the Christian weakness."

"Allah will bless our faith and point the way to his glory," the effendi replies. "The prophet, peace be upon him, has foretold that Rome shall fall."

The red-tinged light of burning homes illuminated the Roman sky. Pope Sergius II viewed Rome's Aurelian wall from his balcony in St. Peter's; he knew it was only a matter of time before the Islamic invaders feasted their eyes on the silver and gold of St. Peter's and St. Paul's Basilicas. Also buried deep beneath the basilica were relics of saints, including that of St. Peter. The pope prayed that these treasures would all remain hidden.

The few Roman auxiliaries made up of Romans, Lombards, and Franks, known as the "Scholae," would not hold back these invading hordes for long. The Aurelian Wall might prevent an assault on the pre-Christian city, but the wealth of Christian artifacts outside the city would more than satisfy the Islamic lust for treasure. Treasures included the golden cross erected above the tomb of Saint Peter and Charlemagne's Silver Altar, adorned with a representation of Constantinople, the capital of the Eastern Roman Empire. Silver plates were also carved with images of the holy family and the saints. A large cross at the basilica's main door, illuminated with over a thousand lit candles, would easily act as a beacon to the invading hordes.

Pope Sergius's heart raced as he witnessed the Roman militia's hasty retreat from Nova Ostia, the port of Rome, to the safety of the Aurelian Wall. Clearly, the eleven thousand Islamic invaders would overwhelm his meager militia.

The commander of the Scholae raced into the room, interrupting Sergius's prayers. "Your Holiness, you must leave now; the infidels must not claim you as their prize. We will secure the main door and place archers in positions that will delay their progress as much as possible. They must pay a price for their arrogance."

Looking with forlorn sadness at the beautiful Silver Altar, Pope Sergius wondered: what about our arrogance?

Present Day
Annapolis, Maryland

Lieutenant Patricia Conway glanced at the ever-growing pile of newly acquired Ottoman references regarding the 1804 meeting between Commodore William Eaton and Viceroy Ahmed Khorshid in Alexandria, Egypt.

"Looks like you have your hands full, lieutenant," Second Lieutenant James Orbani observed while peeking over her shoulder. "I am at your disposal later today if you wish my help to sort out this challenge."

Startled, Conway politely thanked Orbani. She knew of his enthusiasm from her colleagues and welcomed his ability to speak multiple Middle Eastern languages.

"Lieutenant, of course, I welcome any help with this daunting task. I'm due to present my findings to the Annapolis Library in a few days." She smiled at Orbani with a nod toward the pile of papers, hoping he would interpret the gesture as a cue for his departure. Orbani hesitated and, with his well-practiced Lebanese manners, accepted Conway's decline of his offer of help.

Conway's tall, elegant bearing, soft blond hair and polite New England manners invited many admiring glances from her colleagues—some not always welcomed. Her ambition to rise in the ranks and produce her book about America's first war beyond our borders, commonly referred to as "Barbary Wars," was a task she had dreamed of even as a child in Boston. Since 9/11, she often felt compelled to quicken and accomplish this goal.

1804
Alexandria, Egypt

A naval contingent spearheaded by Commodore William Eaton and accompanied by Marine Lieutenant O'Bannon was sent to meet with the Arabs to procure the release of American seamen held as prisoners.

"So, Lieutenant O'Bannon, what do you think of this ancient and beguiling city?" Eaton asked his subordinate from the steps of the British consulate in Alexandria. Eaton, O'Bannon, and a small American delegation were being escorted from the British consulate to the viceroy's citadel.

O'Bannon found himself at a loss for words. As a young naval officer, his current assignment was his first exposure to anything beyond the US borders. For him, Baltimore, Maryland, was the definition of cosmopolitan sophistication. How could he even begin to decipher the sights and sounds of a city like Alexandria, a millennium in the making?

"I take it from your lack of response that you're somewhat overwhelmed," commented Commodore Eaton.

A wry smile crossed over O'Bannon's lips. "Commodore, I'm afraid your observation of my bewilderment is accurate. I hope the Ottoman viceroy doesn't conclude from my expression any lack of resolve in our efforts to free our fellow Americans."

As they approached the citadel, O'Bannon was awed by the scene. The palace was resplendent, illuminated by a long, torch-lit avenue. A large crowd of onlookers stared at them as they passed, curious to see the representatives of the new world. This flurry of activity did little to alleviate his sense of unease.

The viceroy's palace was opulent, with gold-trimmed columns and doors adorned with silver passages from the Koran. Tall, powerful guards stood at attention, regaled in the famed Ottoman style, brandishing steel swords with gleaming gold shafts. O'Bannon looked around and saw dozens of the guards were also mounted on lavishly decorated Arabian stallions.

The commodore and the lieutenant glanced down at their dress uniforms, wondering if the guards were so regal, how must the viceroy appear?

"Lieutenant, I'm beginning to feel somewhat overwhelmed myself," Commodore Eaton confided to O'Bannon.

A loud announcement in what O'Bannon assumed was Turkish was commensurate with the opening of the palace doors. Eaton and O'Bannon were directed to the distant figure of the viceroy, resplendent in recline on an Ottoman couch.

Viceroy Ahmed Khorshid had invited Eaton to call upon him early in the morning. Since it was Ramadan, the holy month of fasting, no refreshments would be offered during daylight hours. But, sensitized to the American's need for some sustenance, the viceroy offered sherbet, coffee, and pipes if the Americans chose to indulge.

Dismissing all from his presence except the two American naval officers, Khorshid observed, "Your visit to my country must be more than mere cultural curiosity."

Eaton replied in French, the language of diplomacy; he addressed the issue of freeing American sailors from the current Bashaw of Tripoli (modern-day Libya). The normal bluntness associated with Eaton's demeanor was deliberately exchanged for subtlety in the hopes of winning the viceroy over to the American plan.

Eaton made the case that Islam and Christianity had much in common, the existence of a supreme being, one God, the forbidding of unnecessary bloodshed. O'Bannon sensed that Eaton was flattering the viceroy, and remarkably, it seemed to be working.

"Viceroy, we are seeking Prince Hamet Bashaw, a legitimate sovereign of Tripoli. He is, as you know, a sovereign loyal to the Ottoman rulers. We wish to restore him to his rightful throne and, in the process, free our countrymen."

"I will grant your wish. I believe he is near Cairo. Please avail yourselves of my offer of a personal escort to Hemet's palace on the banks of the Nile. Lieutenant O'Bannon, I believe you were impressed with my mounted warriors on our magnificent stallions. I hope you enjoy this gesture of friendship, for they will protect you during your trip."

O'Bannon was amazed that his impression of the mounted warriors had so accurately been observed and he could not help but feel that Khorshid sensed his unease and enjoyed his mastery over representatives of the new world, like himself.

Later That Evening
Prince Bashaw's Encampment

The encampment of Prince Bashaw was nestled in a horseshoe-shaped embankment flat with clusters of palm trees along the Nile River. The opulence of the compound challenged the Americans' idea of a military camp. The main tent was silk and trimmed in what appeared to be silver embedded with jewels. The prince reclined on the now familiar Ottoman velvet sofa, with three female attendees busily manicuring and pedicuring to his every whim.

"Commodore." O'Bannon, leaning over slightly, whispered, "If this guy inspires courage and loyalty among his followers, I'd be surprised."

Eaton's droll smile quickly evaporated as the prince motioned his American visitors to recline next to him.

Present Day
Annapolis, Maryland

It was late in the evening and Lieutenant Conway was alone in the library; although she had skipped dinner to accomplish her chosen task, she nevertheless found her curiosity insatiable and had the sense that every discovery added to the mystery and presented another question. The Eaton letters opened a world of imagery. Colorful descriptions of the Egyptian and Ottoman behaviors combined to energize the lieutenant to press on.

Prince Bashaw seemed, according to Eaton, somewhat detached from their discussion of details for the impending mission. While wondering about what now seemed to be a clear portrait of the prince's lack of enthusiasm for granting the American request, her eyes glanced briefly at the name of the Coptic prelate of Cairo: His Holiness, Father Yusuf.

"Why a Christian—albeit Coptic—representative at a military planning session?" Conway asked herself. Once again, her curiosity reenergized her.

In his writings, Eaton described Father Yusuf as diminutive in stature, with a wizened face, much of which was covered by the requisite long gray beard. The commodore wrote about his fascination with a large, ornate gold cross that dangled from the priest's neck, resting on top of the long beard.

Conway realized that her meager knowledge of the Egyptian language was about to be tested. The Coptic prelate kept repeating "Rome's silver," first directly to the commodore, and then in what seemed to be a chant in frustration with of a lack response by O'Bannon. It was clear from Eaton's perplexed expression that neither American knew what the term "Rome's silver" meant.

"I see you're still at it, lieutenant." The voice of Lieutenant Orbani startled Conway. "Can I be of help?"

Attempting to comport herself back from the manuscript to the present moment, Conway replied, "Of course, you may, lieutenant. I didn't mean to imply any indifference earlier to your expertise; for me, this is a challenging language."

"Well then, let's have a go at it." Looking over her shoulder, Orbani pointed to the words of the Coptic priest. "'Rome's silver,' this is curious to me, and I suspect it is to you, too. It certainly seems out of context to their mission. Let's see, as I glance down the diary, it seems as if Father Yusef is saying he knows *where* the Americans can find 'Rome's silver.'"

Conway thought 'Rome's silver' seemed out of context to all the research other historians applied to this era in American naval history.

"Well, I think I'll call this a night; you have been more than helpful, lieutenant," Conway said as she closed her computer and gathered her material. Orbani acknowledged the late hour but departed, saying: "Rome's silver may unlock new insight into your efforts, Lieutenant Conway."

1804
Egypt, the Prince's Encampment

Joining Prince Bashaw's tent in the evening, Coptic Holiness Father Yusef grabbed Lieutenant O'Bannon's sleeve and pointed toward the Nile.

"What is this priest trying to say, and why such urgency?" O'Bannon implored the prince, hoping for some explanation as to what the diminutive priest was trying to communicate.

After an intense exchange in Egyptian between the prince and the priest, which included considerable theatrics on the part of the prince, the prince made a dismissive hand movement and announced, "The priest wants the Christians to know that Rome's lost treasure is guarded and safe in the land of Kush."

"Would you be so kind as to ask his Holiness to elaborate?" Eaton requested.

Present Day
Annapolis, Maryland

Kush—that's modern-day Sudan, Conway thought. Why would a Christian treasure be preserved in what is a well-known Islamic country? Remembering her history of Kush, she knew it was also referred to as Nubia; she had read about its long struggle for its identity under the shadow of Egypt and later its attempt to resist the often-militant expansion of Islam. Conway recalled that Kush had a Christian identity from about AD 350 until AD 900. Could that account for a treasure be referred to as "Rome's silver"? But why the reference to Rome, so far away? Conway realized she had spoken this thought out loud.

Present Day
Khartoum, Sudan

"The infidel Americans are confident they will restore the Christian treasure to Rome. We must not let this happen. Pray that Allah will bless the task before us. I offer my life to prevent this, effendi. I pray that Allah sees fit to make me the instrument of his vengeance." With this statement the Islamic agent ended his coded message from Annapolis to his contact in Khartoum.

Present Day
Annapolis, Maryland

Well, Conway thought, *I need to present my intriguing discovery of 'Rome's silver' to the Navy Book Review committee now—fingers crossed.*

The Navy Book Review Committee

"Lieutenant, as usual your scholarship is impressive. Yet we are not quite certain what you are asking us to do. Could you please explain to the committee what the navy should make of 'Rome's silver'?"

Captain Mark Rossi, speaking for the committee, continued to address Conway. With his professional air, no one would ever suspect that Captain Rossi was attracted to Patricia Conway. He was careful to make sure that his attraction would not influence his recommendation to the committee that followed the meeting. Knowing the lieutenant's enthusiastic demeanor and professional desire to uncover new insight into the navy's early history, Rossi thought of paving the way for Conway to explore and find the key to unlock this silver reference.

Post-Review Committee Recommendation

Patricia Conway was thrilled that the review committee had suggested she continue her research in Rome's Vatican Library.

So, there it was: Rome, the Vatican, her sense of adventure ignited. Rome, for Patricia, was a city of power and mystery—power that shaped the course of European and later world history. Yet, for her, the mystery of this city evoked wonder and a measure of fear.

"I should have never read Dan Brown's *Angels and Demons*," she mused. The mystery always unleashed danger in Patricia's thoughts of Rome.

Present Day
Rome

Patricia Conway found the flight uninspiring, but the view from the plane's window of its descent into Rome quickened her heart. There, for her eyes to examine, were the central physical edifices of Western civilization: the Coliseum, Circus Maximum, the Pantheon, and her destination, the Vatican.

A car picked her up at the Rome airport and brought her to the apartment that Captain Rossi had arranged for her stay in Rome. Conway was curious as to why the captain kept referring to the apartment building as a palazzo. *Wasn't that a term for a palace?* she thought. But after arriving on the other side of the Tiber in Trastevere, any illusion of grandeur was immediately replaced by the sight of a rather run-down, faded, old apartment.

The concierge, a short woman, greeted the lieutenant with a practiced smile at the front door of the palazzo and presented her with a set of keys and an envelope embossed with a symbol of the crown of Saint Peter. The concierge then showed Patricia to her room, which had a small balcony overlooking the Tiber and the cathedral's cupola.

"Signora, should you need anything else, I'm at your service; certainly, it would be my pleasure to help the Holy Father."

"Well, there's no doubt that I'm in Rome. Let's get this letter opened," Patricia uttered out loud.

The concierge, who had said her name was Geena Chiesa, hovered in the doorway before excusing herself. Before she left, she gave a parting glance to the unopened letter, half expecting—or at least hoping—that the letter would be opened in her presence.

Patricia took great care to open the rich and ornate envelope. She hoped it would be an interesting memento of her trip. The envelope contained a brief handwritten note.

Greetings, Lieutenant Conway,
My name is Doctor Francesca Martini, and I am the senior Vatican archivist in charge of antiquities. I've been informed that our services at the Vatican archives should be available to you and your American Annapolis naval colleagues. I look forward to meeting you tomorrow at the Gate of Saint Anne Vatican City at 14:00 (2:00 p.m.).

I'm sure Mrs. Chiesa will suggest a pleasant dining experience for you on your first night in our eternal city.

Sincerely,
Francesca Martini

So, Patricia thought, *Geena is in on the act.* The place was starting to feel like a Vatican/American safe house. "I've been reading too many spy novels, she admonished, needing a rest, "but my stomach and nostrils are calling me to enjoy the pleasures of an Italian dinner."

A stroll along the Tiber succeeded in enchanting Patricia with Trastevere's sounds and hidden streets. The admiring smiles of men confirmed the Italian male ease at communicating pleasure in a women's appearance. *Nice*, she thought. She could get used to this. Not bad for a reserved New England girl!

The next day as Patricia approached St. Anne's Gate, she observed a well-tailored young woman standing by the entrance. Patricia couldn't help admiring the woman's innate sense of style, including her well-tailored silk scarf, an accessory she observed that was common among both sexes in Italy. She glanced down at her requisite American navy uniform and felt intimidated.

As if sensing that she was being observed, the woman approached Patricia and extended her hand. "Signora Conway, I presume. I'm Doctor Francesca Martini. I hope you found everything satisfactory at the apartment." Francesca fell into step with Patricia, and they continued toward the Vatican. Walking down a curving road to the Court of Belvedere, Doctor Martini stopped beside the statue of Hippolytus. "Lieutenant, this is a statue of one of our antipopes."

Patricia looked at the statue. "Does the Vatican memorialize even its antipopes?" she asked.

Francesca smiled. "We have a long history and are aware of our failings, as all humans should be. Hippolytus actually died under ill-treatment, a martyr to his faith, which, as you might guess, went a long way to restore him to the church's good graces."

Suffering for your country at home, you get a medal; here, when you suffer for your faith, you get a statue, Patricia thought. The Vatican might require the United States Navy to erect many statues. Of course, her humor would not be well received by her Vatican host, so she muffled her thought.

A Swiss guard acknowledged Doctor Martini as she approached and opened the door. He pointed to the Tower of the Winds. "Signora, let us ascend these stairs to the Vatican Secret Archives, where we can discuss your mission."

"Francesca—may I call you Francesca?" Patricia asked.

"Please do. I always believed Italians and Americans share a cultural desire not to stand on too much formality. Although, I must admit we Italians can use formality to suit our purposes when need be."

"Well, Francesca, why am I so honored to be escorted to the secret archives?"

"Patricia, you are by our definition neither a journalist nor a photographer. Those two groups are discouraged from gaining access. Scholars such as yourself have been permitted access only since 1881."

"I imagine that there is plenty of material to draw upon."

"Yes, seven and a half miles of material, to be precise. However, not indexed in any orderly fashion. Hopefully for you, we can, using one of your American expressions, cut through some red tape. Remember, we're Italian and not known for efficiency." Francesca smiled slightly.

Patricia wondered if Francesca's self-effacing humor was charming or designed as a back-handed dig at the American sense of efficiency.

They completed the ascent into the narrow and circular Tower of Winds and entered the room called the Meridian; Francesca pointed to an empty desk beneath a large painting of the Sea of Galilee.

"Signor Doctor Julio Benedetto, my colleague, specializing in the church's history in North Africa, has been accumulating all references to the phrase 'Rome's silver.' He and I are quite frankly both stymied. However, our discussion with you might, to use another of your American expressions, trigger off a light bulb."

Patricia smiled at her host. "Actually, Francesca, it's shed some light on the subject, but I like your imagery of the bulb."

"Ah, here he is now."

Doctor Benedetto's appearance immediately confirmed in the lieutenant's mind the universality of the professorial sartorial presentation. He was tall, thin, and wore a tweed jacket with a mismatched tie, very un-Italian. This was the land of *sprezzatura*, where you were expected to make an effortless and beautiful presentation. But Benedetto's warm and charming smile reaffirmed his membership in the world of Italian manners.

Doctor Benedetto made a curt, formal bow and said, "Lieutenant Conway, I'm honored that you and the Annapolis Library have requested our support for your intriguing find. 'Rome's silver' has taxed my and my colleague's expertise. The documents you forwarded to us, the Ottoman references supplied by the Viceroy Khorshid, have required us to look deeper into the Egyptian Coptic Church's exchanges with the Vatican during the first decade of the nineteenth century, which, of course, is the period we are discussing."

Francesca Martini, standing to the side, motioned to Doctor Benedetto that she wanted to add a note of support and some further collaboration.

Francesca looked at Patricia and told her, "We have requested our Vatican office in Alexandra, Egypt, to aid and abet our need for clarification on this matter. They were willing to comply and as such, they are sending us documents supplied by the Coptic chief prelate Father Omar Hassen."

AD 851
Palace of Caliph al-Mutasim

"Effendi, the Makurian representative is here with a peace offering." The servant bowed as he made the announcement and remained in the pose until al-Mutasim waved a dismissive hand at him.

Caliph al-Mutasim recalled the recent humiliation he had experienced after the Christians successfully recaptured the gold mines of Beja along the Nubian Nile. He wondered why the Christian Copt would come to the palace and couldn't imagine what this Christian might want to negotiate.

Zacharias, the son of King George of the Kingdom of Makuria, entered the caliph's inner sanctum. His mere presence annoyed the caliph and the fact that the man strode into the room as if they were equals put al-Mutasim in a dark mood. This man exhibited none of the expected humility of Coptic subjects under the benevolence of Islamic control.

Al-Mutasim cut right to the chase. "What is your offer of peace, Christian?"

"Greetings, Caliph al-Mutasim." Zacharias gave a slight curt bow, more like a nod, and the caliph wasn't sure if he was being mocked. "Your son-in-law, al-Umari, has been defeated by my father, my king. As you are aware, we have regained the gold mines of Beja. We hold your son-in-law as ransom together with the land. The question is, what do you offer us?"

The news of his son-in-law in Christian hands succeeded in visibly withering the caliph's normally vain and robust demeanor.

The caliph eyed his visitor coldly and responded, "If what you say is true, Christian, you will have my answer soon."

10 Hours Later

The caliph's councilors questioned the wisdom of the Christians sacrificing land—a land known for gold and, therefore, wealth and power.

"My son-in-law is a direct descendent of the prophet, peace be upon his name. We will receive Allah's blessing with his return," the caliph told his skeptical council. "We'll offer the Christians the silver and gold taken from Rome's holy sites. They put great value on the ore that has been melted and sculpted into human iconography. They also know they cannot hold the gold mines of Beja for long. Our Muslim numbers grow stronger as theirs weaken. I fear they will murder the descendent of the prophet if I don't agree to their terms."

The room was silent.

Present Day
Vatican City, Rome

"Lieutenant Conway, I have just received a text from my colleague and Coptic Liaison Father Omar Hassen in Egypt. He said that our Coptic breatharians have some references to 'Rome's treasure.' References apparently in the material specifically mention silver and gold. So, if you and Doctor Martini will follow me to my office, we might be able to shed some light on this most intriguing mystery."

Doctor Benedetto held Patricia Conway's elbow and motioned her toward a painting of the holy family. She could tell he was excited about the news he had received from his colleague in Egypt. As Conway approached the painting, she realized it served a dual function as a door.

"Shall we enter, lieutenant?" Benedetto invited as he released her elbow and directed her to the door.

"Please, excuse my sense of wonder, Doctor Benedetto. I'm a bit over-whelmed by what feels like a painting, yet it's a door."

"I take it, lieutenant, that the ornateness of Catholic cathedrals is some-what new to you. You are a Protestant, am I correct?"

"You are, but you would know that from my personnel file forwarded from Annapolis."

"Well, please take no offense from my thoughtless comment. All I wish to do is to act as a guide for you as we approach my business chamber."

Doctor Francesca Martini whispered to Patricia that Doctor Benedetto takes an unusual interest in the many curious art and architectural won-derments of St. Peter's Basilica. She gave Patricia a conspiratorial smile.

"Let us hope he doesn't bore you as well as me. I've heard it all before, with statistics, such as the forty-four alters, twenty-seven chapels, and four hundred statues, all beneath Michelangelo's dome to the depths of the crypt of Saint Peter's tomb."

For Patricia Conway, Doctor Benedetto's office was somewhat of a let-down—nothing ornate, no religious paintings, only a wooden crucifix.

Father Hassen, connecting by Skype to the doctor's computer, looked for an introduction to begin disseminating his findings. Following the formal introductions, Hassen began with an exciting statement.

"I have found a significant historical document that mentions 'Rome's treasure.' Let me begin by showing you an ancient map of the Kingdom of Makuria." A map appeared on the computer screen. "You will note that it corresponds to modern Sudan and overlaps ancient Kush.

"The kingdom, which was Christian, existed when Rome's St. Peter's Basilica was ransacked by Islamic pirates in AD 846. My Coptic colleagues, acting on our behalf, discovered a transaction leading to a territorial exchange between Islamic Egypt and Christian Makuria. As you can see on the screen, Beja was an area in the region where the Nile splits between the White and Blue Nile. It was renowned for its mines that produced gold. The Christians, according to this biased Islamic document, commissioned by Caliph al-Mutasim, realized the recently conquered region of Beja by Christian forces could not be defended and therefore would not remain under Christian rule.

"The document states that silver and gold, referred to as 'Rome's treasure,' was readily accepted by the Makurians for restitution of Beja back to Islamic rule. I'm going to forward these documents to you. Hopefully, Lieutenant Conway, you and your Vatican colleagues can shed new light on this intriguing mystery."

"First of all, thank you, Father Hassen, for your team's hard work. We are indebted to you for providing us with this information. Coptic Father Yusef and Prince Hamet Bashaw acknowledged in 1804 that 'Rome's treasures' were in the land of Kush. When we overlay the map of Kush with that of Makuria, the region of Beja remains well within their boundaries."

Francesca then addressed Hassen: "I seem to recall that the relics of Saint Mark were removed from Alexandria in AD 828. Is it possible that action was done to aid the Coptic Christians?"

"Yes, doctor, your recollection and analysis are correct. Some of us still get annoyed that Venice eclipsed Alexandria as a maritime power with its winged lions. Remember, Saint Mark's martyrdom is in Egypt. The idea that fellow Christians and not Muslims gave away our Coptic heritage is a definite source of irritation. But that is a topic for another discussion."

Recognizing that Father Hassen's visage, even on Skype, seemed a bit perturbed by the insensitive referral to past Christian denominational greed for holy relics, Francesca quickly expressed her regret for her insensitivity to her Coptic contact.

"I ask this," she said, "because it seems that exchanging religious objects between members of different faiths or denominations may have been commonplace during this time. If that is the case, the so-called 'treasures of Rome' might refer to the looted religious objects from St. Peter's in AD 846."

As the conversation evolved, Patricia began to see a possible connection between 'Rome's silver' mentioned by Commodore Eaton in his letters and 'Rome's treasures' ransacked from St. Peter's in AD 846.

Turning to Francesca, she asked, "What silver objects were taken from the Basilica?"

"Well," Francesca replied, "the most famous would be Charlemagne's beautiful Silver Altar. An altar engraved with representations of saints and, most stunning of all, a representation of Emperor Justinian's Basilica, Haji Sofia, in Constantinople. Yes," she shook her head sadly as if a question had been posed, "the same Haji Sofia that was recently converted back from a museum to a mosque."

Francesca and Patricia looked at each other.

"Could it be possible that the Copts, with their close relationship with Constantinople, would value such an altar?" Patricia asked.

Francesca addressed the group. "We seem to feel, judging by the expressions on all our faces, that this prized altar might still exist." There was no response from the group, so she continued. "Speaking for the church, in my capacity as the senior Vatican archivist, if it is out there, we should find it and return it."

Father Hassen cleared his throat and addressed the group. "As I'm sure you already know, European states long ago ended the practice of coveting the material heritage of other countries. It is, in fact, illegal to do so."

"Of course, I take your point, father," Francesca replied, slightly impatient. "My archeological friend Doctor Capitelli and I know only too well your viewpoint."

Hassen inquired further. "Lieutenant Conway, what is the American viewpoint on the proposal of finding this 'Silver Altar'?"

"Well, speaking just for myself, without any direction from Annapolis, I want to find the altar to see if Commodore Eaton's writings were, in fact, valid. Without proof of the existence of the altar we are merely speculating in terms of the final resolve."

"A noble goal, lieutenant, but not necessarily in keeping with the international guidelines that your country follows. And perhaps we should have a plan in place, just on the off chance that the altar exists." Benedetto then suggested they contact their superiors and resume the discussion the next day.

Present Day
On-going Logistics for an Expedition to Sudan

Conway's conversation with Captain Rossi had felt encouraging. The committee had determined that her research thus far warranted a junket to the Sudan to pursue the issue further. But she was surprised and a little uncomfortable that the committee insisted that she include James Orbani in the endeavor. When she questioned the necessity of including Orbani in the group, Rossi told her, "This is not a request—it is a requirement if the trip is to take place."

Conway found the call unsettling. She knew that Orbani's language skills alone made him a perfect addition to the team. But his personality, although pleasant, often seemed somewhat intrusive. A feeling on her part, but in her thus far successful career, she had learned to be attuned to those little nagging feelings.

Well, she thought, *he's coming no matter what I say, and that's that.* Once she had recognized that there would be no Sudan expedition without Orbani, she decided to make the most of it.

Present Day
American Embassy, Khartoum

Captain Rossi had made arrangements with the Ambassador and his team before the group arrived. He had asked the American embassy in Khartoum to apprise the team of any difficult political sensitivities. He also arranged that the team would be met and guided by Thomas Colt, head of the security apparatus at the embassy.

Patricia felt a strange unease: Thomas, when he and she were new recruits in the navy, shared a passionate although brief romance. Obligations to the navy and personal ambitions to rise in their respective careers combined to separate their ardor geographically and emotionally. The thought of him still invoked memories of a passion that hadn't been equaled since. She realized that duty to country, with all that it entails, didn't fill that longing.

She reflected on his physical attributes: Thomas was tall, athletic, with dark wavy hair, a captivating smile, and mischievous eyes with just the right amount of shyness to lure her into his web. Hopefully, she could remain professional and able to resist his charm.

Present Day
Bologna

Marco Capitelli glanced down at his Campari and soda, his favorite afternoon libation, at his favorite bar, Café Neptuno, across from Bologna's famous statute of Neptune. Sitting beside him was his friend and colleague, Doctor of Chemistry Alessio Monti.

Alessio looked at his friend and asked, "Why the smile, Marco?"

"I just received a text from Francesca Martini."

Alessio thought, *well, that explains the smile,* but he said to his friend, "I would have thought that your smile had something to do with your winning soccer kick this morning against those Parma players. That was a deadly shot. What does Francesca want, if I may ask?"

"She wants to meet me tonight here. She is staying at the Hotel Orologio. Apparently, there may be a need, to quote her text, 'a need for my expertise in an alliance with her.'"

"Expertise in a hotel, hmmm. What could she mean?"

"Alessio, that thought is intriguing to me as well." Marco was unable to hide his smile. "She is, foremost, a serious professional. Truth be told, I would like to build on her professional respect. Gaining her respect required an uphill challenge when we first met, so I am gratified that we have continued to stay in touch and that she may need my services."

Alessio looked at his friend, and both men smiled.

That Night
Hotel Orologio, Bologna

Marco arrived earlier than the scheduled time and, per Francesca's instructions, found a secluded table near the hotel's fireplace. Her text had said a secluded table, and he thought she would appreciate the fireplace's classically ornate Greco/Roman carvings.

He wondered why she had never receded in his mind since their last encounter. The answer was made clear immediately as he saw her enter the bar. Her professional authority combined with her beauty affected him as it had the first time they met on the tarmac of Rome's da Vinci Airport almost a year ago.

"Francesca! So good to see you. Can I order you anything from the bar?" Marco stood as she came to the table.

Francesca smiled at him and said, "Why don't you order us the same drink we had at the Hotel Eden that night in Rome?"

"I think we had Negronis, am I correct?"

"Yes, you are; I'm just testing you."

"Is it a test for the early onset of senility?"

"No, I just remember how much you enjoy Negronis, and it brought back memories."

"Good ones, I hope."

"Yes," and again she smiled.

"Francesca, our time together—how should I say this?" Marco looked down at his drink, trying to select his words. "I regretted my clumsy attempt to enter your good graces at the beginning of our assignment in Ethiopia. Your kindness that lovely night on the roof of the Eden went a long way toward my wanting to work with you again and to hopefully rekindle our friendship."

"Do I count this a flirtation from the self-described 'bad boy'?"

"Well, truth be told, yes. I hope it seems more sensitive and mature. I'm still trying to impress you."

"And you're still charming, bad boy. But trying to impress me negates a real impression. Anyway, I see the Negronis arriving. We should get down to business. Let's toast and begin."

Marco once again felt stymied by her intelligent insight into his banter that had previously been so effective with members of her sex.

Moments after Francesca had provided him with an overview of their possible collaboration, he sighed with a plaintive expression.

"Francesca, you're asking me to explore this altar with you in what seems like another dangerous environment."

"I thought you would welcome a chance to demonstrate your skills to solve a historical mystery."

"You missed my point. I was trying to convey my concern about being in dark, closed tombs with you. I don't believe I could control my baser instincts regarding you in such an environment. It was difficult enough last time!"

She looked at him. "Oh, my dear boy, your flirting needs a bit more subtlety, but I appreciate your effort nevertheless."

"It seems I have my work cut out for me." He smiled at her and took a sip of his drink. "Anyway, you want me in Rome for an overview of our mission next week? The answer is yes. I'll be there if only to develop subtlety in your eyes. By the way, what specifically am I looking for?"

"I should have mentioned it sooner. 'Rome's silver'—are you game?" Francesca realized she was distracted from her purpose by this man's mere presence.

"How could I not be?" he replied.

The Following Week

Doctor Julio Benedetto welcomed the newly arrived Second Lieutenant James Orbani. "Your compatriot," he stated with a nod toward Lieutenant Conway, "speaks highly of your language skills. No doubt, our team will call upon those inherent gifts often. You have been briefed as to the, how should I phrase this, 'political and sensitive religious implications of our mission,' I assume."

"Yes, I have, Doctor Benedetto. Briefed is too benign a word. Lieutenant Conway and I have been made highly aware by the US Department of State of the delicacy of our mission. It seems that Boko Haram, the Islamic terror organization, is active in the areas that coincide with our mission."

"I am glad that you know this danger. I see Doctor Martini and Professor Capitelli entering. Please, let me do the honors."

The Americans acknowledged that their government had informed them of the capabilities of their Italian teammates. Patricia, extending her hand to Marco, said with a wry smile that she hoped for an Indiana Jones on this mission.

"Well, signora, excuse me—lieutenant—I'm afraid I'm not as brave as Harrison Ford."

"Maybe not, but you're certainly more handsome. And please, call me Patricia."

"Thank you and call me Marco."

Orbani noticed a tightening expression on Francesca Martini's face. *What is that all about?* he wondered.

Sudan
Khartoum International Airport

"Well, I must say," Orbani observed, "I'm surprised how modern and efficient the airport seems. I think the architectural innovations such as the moving platforms and the informational screens put some of our airports to shame."

"Lieutenant Orbani, the Sudanese welcome these moments of surprise, for they offset what we in Sudan often interpret as Western bias." Orbani was surprised that someone had overheard his off-handed comments. So was the rest of the team.

The Vatican/American delegation turned around in the direction of the originator of the response. A thin, tall, elegant man stood near their group. He introduced himself as Mohamed Sallah, a representative of the Sudanese government. His bearing suggested confidence, and his dark piercing eyes displayed a hypnotic power over others.
After formal introductions were made, he escorted the delegation to the American embassy.

Sudan
American Embassy

Passing the embassy's perimeter, the delegation noticed the guards in combat gear rather than dress uniforms. It seemed appropriate since the embassy was fortress-like and recessed from civilian eyes. While approaching, Patricia began to equate the warnings of Boko Haram with a discernable sense of unease.

"Mr. Sallah," she commented, "this is a bit disquieting. I'm sure you would agree."

"Lieutenant, if you mean the wearing of army fatigues, you should be aware that there have been recent threats made by Boko Haram against all Western interests. Your embassy is just playing it safe. Ah, I see Mr. Colt, head of security, awaiting us at the entrance."

Patricia's heart felt as if it had missed a beat. Thomas Colt looked rakish and deeply tanned and had a soft, welcoming smile on his face, which, in her younger days, would have been hard to resist. She only hoped that the years and her maturity would temper any weakening in her knees.
"Patricia, welcome! You are a sight for sore eyes in this neck of the woods." Colt looked directly at Patricia as if she were the only person in the compound. Conway hesitated for a moment before extending her hand. "Please," Colt said after shaking her hand, "introduce me to your distinguished assembly. Second Lieutenant Orbani," Colt said as he looked at Orbani, "I know of your linguistic skills from Captain Rossi. They will be welcomed, I'm sure, in the days ahead."

Stepping forward, Doctor Benedetto took the initiative to introduce his Vatican colleagues. This is Coptic historian Father Omar Hassen, Doctor Martini of the Vatican Archives, Professor of Archeology and Anthropology Marco Capitelli, and I am Doctor Benedetto representing the Vatican State."

"Welcome," Thomas Colt said. "Let's refresh ourselves with a healthy embassy meal and discuss our mission later."

Later That Day
American Embassy

Thomas Colt, directing the visitors, exclaimed, "So, Doctor Benedetto, if I may sum up for all of our colleagues: the Silver Altar, which was a gift from Charlemagne to the Holy Roman Empire in AD 809, and believed stolen and lost, may still exist according to Sudanese Christian sources, somewhere within the boundaries of the ancient kingdom of Makuria." Doctor Benedetto nodded.

Colt continued to refer to ancient Coptic sources that equated "Rome's silver" with religious processions in and around a Makurian basilica known as Cruciform Church. It was the largest church then and, therefore, most likely to accommodate such a possession. He noted that Cruciform was in the city of Dongola. As he was winding down on his recap of the current situation, he said, "I yield to Doctor Capitelli, who has raised some valid points." With that, Marco rose from his seat and went to the front of the conference room.

"Thank you, Mr. Colt. I have some prior knowledge of this church which I am happy to share. As a student at university, I became aware of the relationship between this church and churches in Ethiopia. Architecturally they have influenced each other. Borders were fluid and as such, Dongola was, during this period of our interest, under the sway of Ethiopia.

"I'm passing you an image of what we think it looked like in the ninth century. Just note we have the original dimensions, and if you glance down, you will notice a current photo supplied by our Sudanese church host. We can barely make out its dimensions. Mohamed Sallah has graciously offered his expertise and service to accompany our mission if only to keep an eye on Boko Haram. That would be enough, but he also has Sudanese archeologists joining us to help with this daunting task."

The Following Morning
American Embassy

Three well-equipped Land Rovers with three Sudanese archeologists and three drivers headed by Mohamed Sallah presented their credentials to the delegation from the West.

"Let me escort these lovely ladies into these rather uncomfortable vehicles," Mohamed Sallah said with what appeared to be a well-practiced smile.

Thomas Colt waited beside a Land Rover. Two vehicles from the American compound pulled up at the end of the caravan, increasing the total to five vehicles traveling to the site. The driver of Thomas's Rover was a member of his security staff, as were the two men traveling in the last car. Colt's Land Rover was positioned second in line in the caravan.

Colt felt a compelling need to address his American security staff and remind them of their duty to represent their country's values even in a hostile country. He wanted to tout their expertise and professionalism but challenge their sensitivity to what could appear as Sudanese hostility or disrespect of their presence.

"You have been chosen for your ability to uphold American values, so believe in what our great country has inculcated into your demeanor. I'll sum it up: respect, professionalism, and strength with kindness." Colt smiled and then motioned the staff to enter the Land Rovers.

Francesca and Patricia went in the third car; Marco, Orbani, and Father Hassen joined Colt in the second car and the rest of the group settled into the remaining space in the other cars, along with the supplies for the trip. Doctor Benedetto remained behind, opting out of the expedition because of prior commitments.

When they were comfortably settled in the car Francesca turned to Patricia and commented that Colt looked like the American actor Kevin Costner. She noted that he had handsome, rugged American looks that appealed to Italian women.

Patricia acknowledged Thomas's female appeal, then quickly commented that Marco captured her idea of the charming and handsome Italian actor, like the love interest of Diane Lane in *Under the Tuscan Sun*.

"Oh, you mean Raoul Bova? Well, I must admit, Marco reminds me of him as well. Like Mr. Bova, Marco's athletic build combined with his graceful charm is hard for me to ignore—let alone that dark brown wavy hair and piecing dark eyes."

"Francesca, it looks like we are drawn to movie stars and handsome men."

Meanwhile, in his car, Thomas turned to Marco. "By my calculations we should arrive at the Cruciform Church in ancient Dongola in about eight hours. Sallah mentioned to me that his men had worked there in the past on related archeological projects. They will sense when and where to begin our work."

"Did he mention the nature of those projects?" Marco asked. "I briefly tried to speak to them in Italian and English, but they didn't seem very knowledgeable; perhaps there was a 'lost in translation' factor in our conversation."

Thomas said, almost to himself, "That's interesting. The Sudanese that normally interact with the embassy are fluent in English." Then he went on at a normal pitch, "The area in question has many Islamic and Christian sites. Apparently, this site has a long history of bringing to light to a modern Sudanese population the cultural imprint of the past."

Cruciform Church, Dongola

Francesca looked at the ancient site with disappointment. "I can't say I see it as particularly thrilling. I'm not certain what I imagined it would be. I am tired from eight long hours in an uncomfortable jeep; maybe that's affecting my receptiveness to this ruin."

"Not very imposing, I agree," Marco chimed. "According to historical records, the church was built on a Kushite queen's treasure trove. By my, although limited experience as well as our recent adventure in Ethiopia, I've learned that churches supplant pagan sites of worship often with holy-think 'treasure-objects.'"

As they began their excavation, the team found that the site presented some curious anomalies: half-submerged columns, some erect and some slanted, all stone-carved scripts corroded and seemingly indecipherable. Most curious to the expedition, in the middle area where the church would be, sat a large, stone-carved lion.

Lieutenant Orbani wondered aloud, "Why a large lion effigy in a Christian church? It seems a bit pagan, don't you think?"

"That's in honor of a queen of Makuria," exclaimed Coptic historian Father Hassen. "Ancient Sudan was able to resist foreign domination due to the heroic leadership of the queen. The symbol of a lioness would not seem inappropriate in their churches. I'll need confirmation, of course, but given the time frame of the Makurian kingdom, this might be to honor Queen Theodora of Byzantine or possibly Saint Anne Faras."

Francesca, leaning into Marco's ear, whispered, "You see, Marco, even the ancient's understood the value and respect for the accomplishments of women."

"Francesca, when will I ever live up to whatever you expect of me?"

"Marco darling, you're making progress—albeit with baby steps."

"Words of encouragement, if ever I heard them, Francesca."

Father Hassen pointed to the burial sites leading to the church. He identified the repetitive black rectangular stones also leading to what appeared to be the entrance to the church—a style that further indicated the Kushite past. Black floor stones were common and extracted from ancient quarries nearby.

Mohamed Sallah directed the expedition to make camp and assemble at the base of a steep ravine in two hours. It did not go unnoticed by the group that his voice and his posture had taken on a new and authoritative demeanor.

American Encampment at the Site

"Thomas, why camp so far from the site?" Patricia asked.

"I don't know," he admitted. "The only thing that comes to mind is a heightened sensitivity to any disturbance of a Sudanese heritage site by ignorant Westerners. My team noticed an attitude change too. Sallah is barking orders to carry our equipment to the site. Thanks for letting me know your observation, Patricia. It's good to be working together." He gave her a look that she wasn't certain how to interpret.

Struggling to ignore her natural attraction to him, she asked, "By the way, what is your opinion of Sallah?"

"My introduction to Mr. Sallah occurred less than a month ago. For two years before that, I had a close inter-government relationship with another Sudanese security chief, Omar Kahib. Why he left and was replaced with Sallah remains a mystery. I have asked our government to investigate the reason and I'm still waiting to hear an explanation.

"I must tell you though, Sallah's current tone with us is a surprise. Perhaps, the barking of orders can be attributed to his need to keep a crew of foreigners in line."

Before Patricia could respond to this line of thought, Marco approached them. Thomas turned toward Marco and said, "You look bewildered."

"Actually, I am, Mr. Colt," Marco said.

"Stop right there, Marco—it's Thomas to you." Colt exhibited a warm, friendly smile. "No formality necessary, especially since we might soon be in dark and dangerous environs together."

"Well, thank you for that vote of confidence. The best way I can explain my facial hesitance is by my limited knowledge of this area, but I know that something is out of kilt."

"Out of kilt," echoed Francesca, now joining in the conversation. "What does that mean?"

Retrieving a compass and a tube of survey maps from his saddlebag, Marco said: "This map, admittedly old, clearly shows the Monastery of the Holy Trinity as within a hundred yards of this site. Yet, it seems to be that Sallah has encamped his entourage in the opposite direction. Why is that?"

Inside a Tent of the Sudanese Contingent

"It is progressing as we had hoped," Sallah stated, his eyes gleaming with the outlook of success within his reach. "The Italian archeologist seems to be questioning our campsite location. So, if we acquiesce to his expertise, it may defuse his issues and bring us closer to our goal. If he continues with his inquiries, we will have to deal with him accordingly. Allah's source among the infidels assures us that the American and Vatican contingent remain unaware of our purpose. Let us submit in obedience to the will of Allah and He will show us the way to deny the Christians their desire."

Sallah's three Sudanese soldiers of Boko Haram, disguised as archeologists, prayed for their success.

Late Evening
American Encampment Site

Francesca and Marco were outside their tents, enjoying the last remnants of the waning campfire.

As they sat enjoying the last vestiges of warmth, Francesca asked Marco, "By the way, a compass and a tube with maps don't seem to be the latest in archeological technology. Is this an homage to Indiana Jones?" She laughed softly to defuse the statement's impact, touched with a bit of flirting.

"Francesca, you of little faith!" He laughed. "And that's saying something of someone who works for the Vatican. I have in my bag of tricks something called a magnetometer whose purpose is to detect how different materials in the ground can cause slight changes in the earth's magnetic field." He smiled at her, and she couldn't help but feel he was being slightly smug.

"Okay, Marco, you have some new, up-to-date toys. I'm going to bed." She kissed him on the cheek and her hand caressed the spot she had kissed. The caress was a fraction of a minute, but her touch lasted for a long time after.

Early the Next Morning
The Monastery of the Holy Trinity Entrance

"Well!" Colt exclaimed to the American contingent. "Sallah's team is de-camping and following our lead. Judging by his expression, it seems that Sallah wants a word with me."

When they met, Sallah referred to himself in the third person. "Mr. Thomas, Sallah must confess that my team's information has relied too heavily on my predecessor Omar Kahib's research documents. It seems to me that your team's archeologist, Dottore Capitelli, has a deeper af-finity for this endeavor. So, perhaps you and your team should lead the way."

Thomas returned to the group and announced, "We're heading out."

"Thomas," Patricia asked quietly, "you look puzzled. What gives?"

"I'm not sure, Pat, but something is not lining up."

He turned to the group and said, "So, Marco, where do we start?"

"I'll use my magnetometer, which Francesca has dubbed my new toy," Marco replied, glancing at Francesca. "It should indicate a hollow area in this immediate vicinity. Then, if it is so, we should begin digging. If my calculations are correct, the passageway leading to the Cruciform Church from the monastery will become accessible for exploration."

"Let's begin," Thomas shouted.

Hours Later

"Well, Professor Capitelli, what progress are we making?" Sallah inquired with thinly disguised impatience.

"I can say my magnetometer keeps indicating a hollow area beneath the area that we're standing now. According to your predecessor Kahib's documents, there is an indication of a pool of water not far below. And even more curious, a systemic decline evenly distributed and repeated beneath the water. It suggests to me something man-made, like steps. I suggest that you order your men to start digging here. By the way, from all appearances, your predecessor did good research."

Marco turned and walked away. He didn't see Sallah scour at him.

A short time later, water was discovered no more than a few meters below them, and steps of stone were visible approximately two feet beneath the water.

Marco asked Francesca to hand him his travel equipment. Moments later a diving mask and oxygen tank appeared, and Marco suited up with the requisite fins. Francesca couldn't help but giggle and say, "Cute!"

"Well, wish me luck before I go in and attach this rope to my waist. I'll tug on this once to say I'm fine and twice to say I need to return to the surface."

Lieutenant Orbani commented, "If steps are here, there may be inscriptions that need deciphering or translating. I can join you and perhaps Sallah can supply me with some diving equipment. Professor, could you use my help?"

"Of course. I'm always in need of assistance; thanks for the offer. Lieutenant Orbani, you might as well suit up. Hopefully Francesca won't tease you."

Orbani's and Marco's descent was over in moments. The two dove into the pool and kicked downward alongside the visible steps using their hands to pull them along. Since the water was fresh their eyes didn't sting as they would have in salt water. They lost natural light as they descended and used their illumination equipment proportionally. Marco motioned to Orbani that the man-made steps began to rise, leading to what was an opening to an underground cave above the water line. After that, the men broke to the surface.

Startled, they absorbed a vast man-made carved subterranean chamber. As it was enshrouded in darkness, they knew that investigation would require high-powered light sources. A figure loomed ahead but remained indistinguishable—could it possibly be a statue?

Orbani said, "I'll ask Sallah to send lighting equipment and additional help in the exploration."

That Evening
Sallah's Tent

"Allah is paving the way for our success." Turning to his Sudanese team, Sallah ordered them to descend and await "our moment of triumph."

We, Allah's servants, must wipe out the Westerners' belief in their false sense of superiority.

The American Team That Evening

As they sat by the fire's dying embers, Thomas turned to Patricia. "Sallah claimed his maps, afforded to him by his predecessor, did not accurately indicate where to begin the dig. However, my map, which Marco is using, is the same one Mohamad Kahib made available to our embassy. The question is, why the discrepancy? And why now? I need to get down there with some of our men to see what's up."

Patricia looked at him. "Promise me you'll be careful."

"I will, Patricia." Colt felt an internal warmth unleashed by Patricia's comment and care.

Trying to bring the conversation back to a more professional level, she added, "I would suggest, given their expertise, that you ask Francesca as well as the Coptic Father Hassen to participate."

"Of course, Patricia, you are reading my mind. That's a gift of yours that I remember so well." He looked at her wistfully. "But that's a conversation for another time." Holding his gaze on Patricia a bit longer than usual, he abruptly rose and said he was turning in. The next day would be long.

The Next Day
The Excavation Site

The Sudanese, American, and Italian teams linked up in the subterranean chamber. After disrobing their diving equipment, they turned on the high-powered lighting equipment and aimed the device at the dark archway. The revelation of what appeared was startling. A statue of a woman in regalia, certainly a queen, seemed to require the team's fidelity. Her outstretched hand, for lack of a better word, called for genuflecting to continue their exploration.

Turning to Francesca, Marco exclaimed, "Seems to me no matter where you go, women are in charge."

"Well, Marco, you are showing wisdom after all."

"Thanks, Francesca—I think."

Moving closer to examine the statue, Marco discerned the name Kandake. "What does the name mean?" Francesca asked.

"Well, Kandake is the title for all Kush queens. As you know, Makuria is the kingdom that supersedes Kush. The Latin term for Kandake is Candace."

Sallah motioned that the team should proceed without unnecessary delays. They needed to be mindful that power sources had to be used sparingly.

A long-carved passageway sloped slightly down, resplendent with Kushite figures, combining human form and animal features. As the team approached what was believed to be the border of the Cruciform Church, the first Christian symbol appeared, a statue of Saint Mark in Egyptian Coptic regalia. Father Hassen translated the inscription as a call for repentance before entering a sacred site.

The explorers walked under a huge arch that seemed to lead into a wide circumference hall. There seemed to be no immediate exit upon first inspection. An alcove set to one of the sides quickly caused the team to assess the hall as not a circular room but rather a rectangular structure. The effects of geographical sedimentation have had their way of reconfiguring the architect's original intention.

The team approached the alcove and marveled at the worn but still stunning reliefs of Christian symbols. As the explorers approached the reliefs, they felt a perceptible drop in temperature. The cooling effect seemed to be attributed to a gradual decline and the revelation of more steps descending to the right of the relief.

Francesca quickly began interpreting the relief as a pictorial representation of Mary and Joseph's journey to Egypt. She described an angel, seemingly directing the holy family toward the many newly noticed steps.

Sallah, showing his now customary impatience, called out loud for less relief analysis and quicker exploration.

Colt turned to his American and Vatican explorers to heed the Sudanese's directive. The steps beneath seemed endless. Descending felt damp and the steps were wet and released a faint crunch with each descent.

Patricia felt the claustrophobia she remembered from a class trip to the Mayan temples in the Yucatan.

Moments later, another oblong vestibule with high ceilings and ornate columns styled as Ethiopian obelisks presented itself.

Marco, turning to Francesca, exclaimed, "Ethiopian obelisks! Déjà vu and a bit unsettling—isn't it, Francesca?"

"My thoughts exactly. Finding another Italian Army priest in prison seems unlikely, don't you think?" She smiled at him, and he smiled back.

At that moment, Patricia interrupted their conversation down memory lane with her extended arm pointing to small skeletal figures dressed in what appeared to be religious garb. Human skulls with empty eye sockets seemingly smiled at the new visitors.

"They seem to be guarding an entrance." She pointed to a darkened opening no more than a yard behind them.

"But an entrance to what?" Thomas whispered to Patricia.

Approaching the entrance, it was necessary to touch the skeletal figures to move them so the team could proceed into this part of the oblong vestibule.

Sallah rushed forward with his crew and pushed hard against the religious figures, toppling a few.

Father Hassen voiced his displeasure with their insensitive action, apparently to no avail.

"We need to absorb this area since there is a faded mural, and before your men toppled these religious guardians, we need to pause and be a little reflective. These guardians were pointing to the mural to the right of the entrance portal," Francesca exclaimed in her practiced commanding voice that is often required to protect and discern valued Vatican artifacts.

Sallah reluctantly acquiesced.

Thomas whispered into Patricia's ear, "I think for all his bravado, Sallah had a commanding mother. Wouldn't you say?"

Patricia laughed, "No doubt, Thomas, no doubt at all."
It was good to hear Patricia laugh; it lightened his heart.

The mural, faded as it was, revealed a well-known story of the origins of Christianity in Ethiopia and Kush. Hassen excitedly pointed to the conversion of the eunuch from the court of Queen Candace of Ethiopia. "This is the earliest representation that I have ever come across. It identifies Philip—not the apostle but the disciple, following the order of an angel to head south of Jerusalem. You can see that Philip quotes Isaiah 53:7–8. *"He was oppressed, and he was afflicted, yet he opened not his mouth; like a lamb that is led to the slaughter."*

Turning to Francesca, Father Hassen asked, "What could this mural suggest to you, Signora?"

"Well, besides its historical intent, the church seems afford a sense of importance to this location. If that is the case, we could be entering a location containing items that enhance and support the Christian faith. Certainly, a Silver Altar would support that faith."

One of Sallah's men overheard Francesca's response and immediately sought out his effendi.

A few yards farther, the entrance widened, revealing a well-constructed vestibule. Ornate columns featured religious inscriptions. Damp air filled the nostrils of the explorers and a musty odor of decay intensified as the team reached the center of the vestibule.

"There don't seem to be any additional passageways that I can see." Thomas Colt addressed the explorers. "Maybe, Marco, you can decipher some of these inscriptions and encourage us to continue. As of right now, it appears we are at a dead end."

Sallah, in his now customary forceful voice, exclaimed, "Let us hope with all your Western expertise we have something to justify our efforts."

Marco, exhibiting a look of disappointment, turned to Francesca, stating, "Nothing on these columns points to any reference of a Silver Altar. I've turned 360 degrees and I'm not turning up anything. What say you, Francesca—any clues?"

"I think we need to ask ourselves: did we unintentionally leave something out?"

"For the life of me, I can't think of what. Maybe you can call on your female intuition and pick up what may have been overlooked."

A beautiful smile combined with a wink in Francesca's eye was quickly accompanied by her head nodding to the floor beneath.

"The floor, of course, the floor! What do we look for? I'll answer that myself; there can still be inscriptions."

Raising his voice for all to hear, Marco ordered the participants to look for any markings beneath them.

The floor stones were interlocking mosaics, each with faded blue trims. Colt and Sallah directed their crews to look for any anomalies. Their movements raised clouds of dust that had been undisturbed for centuries. Irritable eyes and coughing were the by-products of their efforts.

Covering her mouth with a scarf, Patricia Conway noticed a stone mosaic larger than the others. She immediately called out to Marco to investigate.

As he stood over the circular stone, Marco's eyes fell upon a Coptic inscription. He asked Father Hassen to translate the inscription.

Marco's heart skipped a beat upon hearing Moretti's translation.

"In the realm of prayer and stone an altar of Rome awaits."
Marco read the translation out loud, elevating his voice to gain the attention of the expedition.

Sallah quickly ordered his crew to gather by the Coptic inscription and exclaimed, "We must break this stone now and see what lies beneath."

"No, wait," Marco responded. "I suggest that we consider that this stone is not concealing a hidden room housing the altar, but it calls upon us to use our discernment of the 'realm of prayer and stone' phrasing as a clue to unlocking a hidden portal somewhere in this very room."

"Signore Capitelli, I believe you are stalling for time when the answer lies directly below us."

Injecting his opinion, Colt said, "Look, Sallah. Let's give Marco the courtesy of at least testing his theory."

"Very well then, but my patience and that of my men grows short."

In unison, Thomas and Francesca turned to Marco, saying, "The magnetometer."

"Francesca, you want me to use my new toy again? Well, you're right; if there is anything hollow beneath this stone, we'll know."

Moments Later

"It is solid material with no indication of any hollow anomaly," Marco declared.

Turning to the Sudanese contingent, Colt said, "Well then, Sallah, let's cool our jets and give our archeologist Doctor Capitelli the time he requires."

"Your American expressions, 'cool our jets,' humorous, no doubt, to you, are disrespectful to us. Nevertheless, let the doctor proceed."

Marco quickly surveyed the religious site. Considering the personnel at his disposal, he divided them into groups of three and ordered the explorers to slowly run their hands against the walls. His intent was for all carvings or seams to present themselves.

One of the American contingents called out to Colt, "What is this white material alongside this wall?"

Thomas called Marco over and lifted some of the material to discern.

Marco responded, "Upon first examination, there is a bit of a glow. I'll taste it. I believe it's phosphorus."

"Calcium, Marco?"

"More likely the white bone residue of workers. Have your men press along this section, Thomas. There may be a shifting of the wall. It's an educated guess, but men seemed to labor along this wall with tools for a purpose."

Sallah's men rushed over and applied their numbers, along with the Americans, to press against the wall. The white bone material slowly shifted and diminished into a tiny but slowly enlarging gap.

Marco called for an illuminating probe to snake its way through the gap. Moments later, he discerned a semi-half-moon-shaped room. Probing farther, this room appeared to resemble a part of a church where a priest could conceivably hold a service.

"What do you see, Doctor Capitelli?" Colt asked.

"Doctor Capitelli? Why suddenly the formality, Thomas? What happened to Marco?"

"Forgive me, Marco. I'm just excited to know."

"Okay then, I see what may suggest an altar. Let's breakthrough now. You're not the only one excited."

Within Minutes

A portal large enough to walk through, or more precisely crawl through, presented itself.

Sallah edged closer with his men and urged Marco to enter within. The room could hold no more than eight people, at best.

As the inner chamber was illuminated, a stone-carved altar emerged.

"What is it, Marco?"

"It's an altar, just not silver. Nevertheless, have all the crew enter after you have widened the portal. I think there is more here than what meets the eye."

Sallah, with a thinly disguised disdain, suggested that Doctor Capitelli was wasting everyone's time in this dead-end endeavor.

"With all due respect, Signor Sallah, it's not my desire to waste your or anyone else's time. I am an archeologist and still believe there is more to learn."

Interjecting with his raised voice, Colt advised, "Sallah, let him be the professional we know him to be and give him the respect due."

Patricia whispered to Francesca, "His assertiveness reminds me of why I found him so attractive."

"I can see why, Patricia," Francesca replied.

Examining the altar closely, Marco's hands slowly searched for any anomaly. If he detected anything, his team could not see or imagine what was transpiring in his mind.

Calling for Francesca and Father Hassen, Marco then asked if the faded mural of Saint Mark hovering over the stone altar suggested anything to them.

Speaking first, the father said the saint's eyes were looking at the altar rather than the usual blank outward stare. Francesca concurred and added that Saint Mark was smiling as well, which was also unusual.

Marco thanked them, and turning to both, he asked, "What knowledge does the Vatican have of the actual dimensions of the Silver Altar?"

"Well, by our limited knowledge," Francesca said, "the altar is said to be two and a half feet by eight feet in diameter."

"Thank you. Now let's measure this stone altar. Three feet by nine feet. Francesca, do the smiling Saint Mark and the similar dimensions suggest anything to you?"

"Yes, it does. What do these stone chips mean to you, Marco?"

"Well, they would indicate carvings by tools, possibly used to hold up an altar."

Calling for Thomas to gather his men around the altar, Marco requested that the magnetometer be applied to the stone altar.

Thomas asked, "What material is indicated beneath the stone surface?" Looking up, Marco quietly stated, "It's silver!"

"Silver!" Thomas exclaimed, his voice at a high pitch. Intentionally or not, he succeeded in gaining the attention of all the explorers. Rushing ahead, Sallah ordered his men to attempt to break the stone altar.

Looking at Sallah with undisguised scorn, Marco and Thomas questioned the wisdom of immediately destroying the altar before discerning a less invasive way of accomplishing the task.

"It seems we may prevent some unnecessary destruction to accomplish our goal. Why settle on breaking what is at least a part of Sudan's Christian heritage, even if there is no silver beneath?" Marco asked.

Marco further postulated that if the Silver Altar was beneath the stone, the worshippers might have thought of a way to expose the altar for rare and safe occasions while under Islamic persecution.

"I'll acquiesce for now, Westerners," Sallah grumbled. "Just know I'm not a patient man."

Thomas, leaning toward Patricia, whispered, "Not a patient man? You could have fooled me."

Turning again toward Marco, now joined by Patricia and Francesca, he asked the group: "Any encouraging ideas?"

Marco's expression lacked his customary bravado, replaced with what Francesca thought was a new humility of uncertainty. Her desire to hug him was a new feeling for her.

Patricia did not fail to observe Francesca's changed demeanor, saying, "Well, we like our guys when they assert themselves, and may we add to also when they express humility?"

Nodding in agreement and accompanying the gesture with a smile, Francesca replied silently.

"I'll welcome all ideas; to tell the truth, I'm a bit stymied," Marco responded. "The last time, Francesca, you winked and smiled, looking at the floor. Can you work your magic again?"

"How would an altar of stone be lifted?" she responded.

"By a pulley system, I imagine."

"Then where would that system be attached?" Smiling, she glanced at the ceiling above.

"Am I deceiving myself or is there a stone-carved hook directly above this altar?"

"There is, there is," Colt exclaimed. He immediately ordered a crew member to return to the surface and bring the equipment necessary to perform the task.

Later

Hooking up the steel-enforced pulley to the four corners of the stone altar proved easier than originally thought. Getting the correct leverage to pull on the line in a small tight environment was another matter altogether.

Colt ordered his three-man crew to pull from the larger adjacent vestibule. Their first efforts proved futile. Sallah called on some of his crew to support the effort. Then, with the sound of rumbling, the stone lid seemed to move, releasing long trapped dust and, oddly, a hint of wind. All involved gasped as a still-stunning Silver Altar illuminated the dark alcove.

Shouting in Arabic, Sallah gave a command to his men. His voice broke the alluring spell of the still beautiful Silver Altar. The Italians and

Americans turned to see Sallah's men aiming their previously hidden firearms at them.

Sallah, with a pistol in hand and raised voice, commanded: "Please, Doctor Capitelli, move away from this Christian blasphemy. I want you to witness the destruction of your false icon. Regarding the rest of you, I suggest you move out of this enclave and my men will tell you where to stand. Yes, they're my men, not the Sudanese government's men. We are Boko Haram.

"You must not believe blasphemers that you could have succeeded in your goal. Allah has chosen Boko Haram as the instrument of his vengeance."

Colt calmly asked Sallah to let the innocent explorers go free. "Since you will destroy the altar, they will be unable to exploit this discovery. We, however, are not innocent in your warped eyes."

"One of 'your men' is innocent in Allah's eyes, and right now, his pistol is aimed at Lieutenant Conway." Sallah smiled.

Thomas turned, quickly losing his calm demeanor, and saw Lieutenant Orbani's pistol aimed at a now-shaking Patricia.

"You seem so shocked, Colt. Orbani has always been Allah's instrument of your defeat. We have known of Conway's research into Commodore Eaton's letters of Rome's Silver from the beginning. Now, and I won't ask again—Doctor Capitelli, move away from the altar."

Marco's eyes searched desperately for Francesca, who was being led out at gunpoint with Hassen and the American contingent. He backed away and went to stand next to Colt. Marco turned to him and whispered, "Any chance of a rescue by the calvary?"

"Silence!" Sallah roared.

Orbani moved Patricia toward Sallah's followers and stood alongside Sallah, his gun aimed at Colt and Capitelli.

"You have been defeated, Christians. I suggest you—"

Mid-sentence, Orbani turned his gun and placed it at Sallah's temple. Sallah's shocked expression was enhanced by the clicking of pistols in the adjoining outer vestibule.

"It seems, Sallah," Colt said, smiling with relief, "that Second Lieutenant Orbani is not one of yours after all—but a loyal American naval officer."

"You forget, Colt, I have all my men with guns awaiting my orders to execute you infidels."

"The clicking you heard, Sallah, is not the guns of your men, but yes, they are Sudanese. They are the men of Omar Kahib, your esteemed predecessor. You see," Colt continued, "we have known about your plans for a long time. Lieutenant Orbani infiltrated Boko Haram and was planted as our double agent. We needed the cooperation of the Sudanese government and Omar Kahib and they have been exceedingly cooperative as they are aware of Haram's corruption of the tenets of Islam."

Almost on cue, Sudanese Security Chief Omar Kahib entered the altar alcove, claiming: "Your men have been disarmed, Sallah." Orbani grabbed Sallah's gun taking advantage of his stunned expression.

"How did you get down here undetected?" Sallah growled.

Colt responded for Kahib. "From the start of the expedition to the Cruciform Church, Kahib's men have followed close behind and when I sent one of my men up for the pulley, he returned undetected—because you would not question our action when that same action would benefit your purpose."

Kahib spoke directly to Sallah, saying, "Islam is a religion of peace, but you have highjacked it for your purposes of power."

Sallah, visibly agitated, screamed, "Why give the Christians their victory?"

"We will not live up to the prophet—peace be upon his name—until all Sudanese citizens can worship in peace."

"But the Christians will parade their victory for all to see in Rome!"

"No, Sallah. But I think you should hear it from them."

Francesca and Father Hassen entered the room. Marco and Francesca looked at each other with undisguised relief and affection.

Francesca answered for the Vatican. "It's our hope that this discovery will remain here so that the minority Coptic Christians will have a symbol of their faith and its endurance here. The Sudanese government has assured the protection of this site."

Sallah and his men were led away. Marco embraced Francesca. Immediately, Patricia and Thomas mirrored them.

"You see, Marco," Colt explained, "the calvary has arrived."

A Few Days Later
The Hotel Eden Rooftop, Rome

"It was lovely of you to invite me to share my last evening with you, looking out over your seductive Rome, Francesca," said Patricia.

"Patricia, it's a new tradition that Marco and I started after our first adventure together in Ethiopia. It seems to me that you should share in that tradition."

"I'd like to add one more person tonight," Patricia responded. "But alas, he was called back to Washington. I didn't have the chance to tell him how I felt seeing him again. It seems fate and obligations have conspired against us. I learned later that Captain Rossi and the Annapolis brass were aware of Thomas's undertaking since I uncovered Commodore Eaton's correspondence.

"So where is Marco? Is he on another adventure, and did you have time to tell him how you feel?"

"Actually, he is joining us shortly. He has some sort of previous obligation, or so he claims." Francesca looked toward the doorway. "Oh, speak of the devil."

Greeting the women with a kiss on both checks in the Italian manner, Marco sat and motioned for the waiter. He ordered a Negroni and a refill for the drinks of his companions. "I apologize for my tardiness. Please let me order for you if you wish. I can recommend many of their dishes, particularly pappardelle Bolognese. Being from Bologna, I know a thing or two about food."

Francesca's eyes rolled with a faint smile, thinking: *Parma and Bologna; will they ever compromise on culinary differences?*

"Again, let me thank you for sharing your tradition here at this beautiful hotel," Patricia repeated. "I only wish Thomas was here to share it with us."

Francesca interrupted, "I think you should look over your shoulder—your drink is here."

"I didn't order a drink; why is it here?" Turning her head, she saw Thomas standing behind her.

She couldn't hide her pleasure. "So . . . that was Marco's previous obligation, I see! Did it take any arm-twisting to get you to come?" Patricia asked him.

Marco and Francesca stood and excused themselves and left the table.

"None whatsoever." Taking Patricia's hand, Thomas proclaimed, "I will not let this chance pass without telling you how much you mean to me and letting you know that I hope to win your love."

The Americans embraced and Marco and Francesca looked deeply into each other's eyes.

The Blue Nile Blues

BLUE NILE BLUES Major Characters

Biruk Arega: Chief engineer of the Ethiopian Renaissance Dam

Assefa Berhane: Assistant Director of Ethiopian Antiquities

Aamina Gebremichael: Director of Ethiopian Antiquities

Zala Aron: Ethiopian doctor of symbology

Carlo Monti: Italian ambassador to Ethiopia

Antonio Forte: Italian Minister of International Economic Development

Marco Capitelli: Professor of archeology and anthropology

Francesca Martini: Senior Vatican art director and archivist

Professor Guerci: Head of Bologna's department of archeology

Thomas Magnani: Professor of geology, Rome University

Aldo Manfredi: Chief Italian military engineer

Hu Lee: Chinese planning commissioner for the Renaissance Dam

Xin Chin: Doctor of archeology and architecture, Milan University

Lieutenant Khan: Egyptian helicopter pilot

Count Farnese: Italian national hero, archeologist,
 and mentor to Marco Capitelli

METEC: (Ethiopian) Metals and Engineering Corporation

THE BLUE NILE BLUES

PROLOGUE

In the fifteenth century, Ethiopian Emperor Lalibela commissioned a series of churches to be cut into solid rock. Rather than being built from the ground up, cutting into the earth created impressive churches of solid rock in the shape of the Christian cross.

In his planning, the emperor selected the highlands with its vast plateau as the area best suited geologically for creating the churches. Islam surrounded Ethiopia in the fifteenth century, as it does today, and for the Ethiopians, the highlands afforded unassailable physical protection to their faithful. The churches served as a religious testimony to Ethiopia's adherence to the Coptic Christian faith. To that end, certain features were incorporated into the churches themselves. The churches included large paintings and murals of the biblical prophet Enoch, the great-grandfather of Noah. The emperor believed Enoch protected the faithful and the emperor intended to include the protection of his people in the building of the churches.

Renaissance Dam

Chief engineer Biruk Arega's eyes scanned his weekly summation report to the Ethiopian prime minister on the project's status. He knew that the words he chose to describe the Grand Renaissance Dam, which would supply electrical power to sixty million recipients, hid the truth of the malignant corruption embedded in the project. The dam was the national pride of Ethiopia and Biruk Arega was responsible for overseeing this vital project's construction. His conscience could no longer allow him to be silent on this matter. This weekly report would tell the truth. Yes, it was time that the truth be known. He hit the Send button on his computer.

The sound of the drilling machines had ceased hours ago. Normally, Biruk welcomed the silence, but tonight, alone in his cavernous underground office, he sensed an uninvited presence.

Turning around quickly and peering into the dark hallway behind him, he saw a distant shadowy figure emerge. Recognizing the approaching figure, he permitted himself a smile of relief.

"It's you," he said.

The Grand Ethiopian Renaissance Dam Conference
Addis Ababa, Ethiopia

As the prime minister approached the dais, he glanced at his wife sitting in the audience. She was surprised to see an expression of fear and apprehension on his face; it was subtle and would not be noticed by anyone else. She could not recall in their storied romance any fear in her husband, even during their years as freedom fighters against Ethiopia's military dictatorship.

But now his face, aged and wizened by dark circles under his eyes, which begged for sleep, caused a tear in her eye.

The prime minister addressed the audience: "The sincere attempt by our country to gain 6,000 megawatts of electricity and double our country's power supply has become a national and international embarrassment."

The Ethiopian prime minister paused to consider his next words. "In light of the recent suicide of the dam's chief engineer, Biruk Arega, and the growing evidence of corruption in our military-industrial conglomerate known as METEC, I have decided after consulting with my advisers to disband METEC immediately. Further, I have decided to open the engineering requirements to foreign participation. This project is too important to our country; we cannot let it fail."

Beijing
Communist Party Belt and Road Planning Commissioner

"As you know, our Belt and Road Initiative is designed to give us access to less developed nations to promote our Chinese hegemony. Although we reached out to the Ethiopians with their Renaissance Dam project by our substantial funding of METEC, it seems the Ethiopian prime minister has chosen without consulting us to dismantle METEC." He paused to let this news register with this audience, then continued. "Needless to say, China's influence to promote our country's goal of supplanting the West's commercial dominance is at risk."

The speaker, Hu Lee, lowered his gaze to the men and women assigned to carry out the task of expanding China's glory in Ethiopia. When he raised his eyes again and looked at them, he accompanied it with a loud command for those same men and women to sing China's national anthem. No one in the room disobeyed his command.

Cairo
Egyptian Power and Energy Commissioner

"As you know, the Nile is a shared resource between our country, Sudan, and Ethiopia. Our people see the Nile as their source of life. As our population has risen, the water supply for our people has fallen."

The commissioner paused, looked around the room to gauge the attention of his audience, then continued. "Ethiopia must fill its reservoir slowly and release water carefully so the Nile's flow is not disrupted, especially during droughts. This is important during this unsettling period of climate warming. The Aswan Dam has benefited Egypt and our neighbor Sudan, and Ethiopia must follow our example.
I am reminding all of you of this because I have, in my possession, a written transcript from my friend and counterpart in Ethiopia, Biruk Arega. It was sent right before his untimely death." He paused. "Most disturbing." The commissioner waved the paper in his hand but didn't divulge the contents.

Unknown to the commissioner, a staff member in the pay of China took note.

Rome
Office of Antonio Forte,
Italian Minister of International Economic Development

"I've called this hasty meeting of our various departments to inform you of a sudden and unexpected opportunity for Italy to become involved in Ethiopia's Grand Blue Nile dam project. METEC, the military-industrial conglomerate spearheading this project, has been disbanded. Details of this disbandment are sketchy at best, but corruption in its many forms is certainly at play. The bottom line is the Ethiopians are looking for new partners. So, this floor will be open tomorrow at this time for your input on how Italy can offer its assistance."

Several Days Later

Marco Capitelli sat in the Zoom conference call with a group representing the Italian government and a delegation from the Renaissance Dam project; he was amazed at how quickly Antonio Forte had been able to get the meeting organized. But then, Marco knew a newly developed friendly relationship had come together after the Italians and the Ethiopians had been involved in a joint project in Ethiopia.

Assefa Berhane, the Assistant Director of Ethiopian Antiquities who had been part of that joint project, directed her question to Antonio Forte, the Italian Minister of Economic Development.

"Antonio, my friend, it is a pleasure to see you again. It seems we Abyssinians need some help with our dam project, and since our last meeting with you and your team was so successful, we thought a conversation with you would be a good place to start. I think you and your team are fully up-to-date on our Blue Nile project. And I'm sure you're aware that we have severed our ties with METEC."

"Assefa," Forte replied, "just seeing you brings a smile to my aging face; of course, with this Zoom meeting, you might mistake the smile for my ever-increasing wrinkles."

"Wrinkles—that's not possible, my dear friend. But let's get to the matter at hand. We need your expertise to build this huge undertaking. Does your government have a plan to help us?"

"Well, we have some thoughts, albeit in the early stages. So, along those lines, I would like to turn the screen over to Professor Guerci, head of the University of Bologna's archeology department."

"Thank you for this opportunity to help with your project, a project that benefits all in your region, not just Ethiopia." Professor Guerci appeared on the screen wearing his signature bow tie.

"I have given this request some thought and have already taken the liberty of formulating a team, including one member with whom you already are familiar, Professor Marco Capitelli."

Before Professor Guerci could continue, Assefa Berhane interjected, "Of course, we remember Professor Capitelli's outstanding contribution to resolving that difficult chapter between our two countries, and we would be delighted to work with him again. But he is, as I remember, an archeologist, not an engineer. Am I correct?"

"Yes, it is true that engineering seems to be the primary focus of Ethiopia's dam project. However, we submit that damage to some of your ancient heritage sites may occur within the scope of the project and we feel that it can be prevented with a little planning."

"Well, yes, that possibility exists, Professor Guerci. But our engineers indicate the circumference of the newly created water reservoir will not damage any existing heritage sites. And, to be honest, this issue with METEC has put us considerably behind schedule."

"Signora Berhane," Antonio Forte said, injecting himself into the conversation, "if you would allow me to direct your attention to a high-residue satellite image of the area in discussion. Notice that it reflects many gradations of color. The darker the color, the deeper the soil depth. If I can turn over the screen to Professor Thomas Magnani, Italy's premier geologist, he can explain the significance of this finding."

Signor Magnani, trying hard to avoid scientific minutia, presented a brief explanation of the significance of the darker soil colors. He told the group that an ancient dried underground riverbed was beneath the proposed lake of the dam project. This, he told the group, was significant because the now-dormant riverbed could easily be reactivated, and then ancient heritage areas beyond the immediate lake region could be in jeopardy.

Beijing
Office of Hu Lee,
Commissioner of China's Belt and Road Initiative

"Comrades, our sources indicate the Italian incursion into our engineering initiatives regarding the Renaissance Dam are being received favorably by the Ethiopian authorities. I suggest we remind those Ethiopians who have benefited from China's largess to see that the West, in this instance Italy, does not succeed."

Addis Ababa
Office of Aamina Gebremichael,
Assistant Director of Ethiopian Antiquities

"Carlo Monti, so good to greet you as Italy's ambassador to my country." Aamina Gebremichael reached out her hand to the handsome man standing before her.

With his customary broad smile, Ambassador Monti replied, "Aamina, thank you. It is truly a pleasure seeing you again. And I am delighted that you have had a well-received promotion to director of Ethiopian antiquity. Congratulations."

"One that matches yours from undersecretary to the ambassador. We have done well since we last met two years ago and participated in the rapprochement between our two countries.

Now it seems our governments are calling on us to call on some of our old friends to accomplish a dam project that will benefit my country and our regional neighbors, Sudan and Egypt."

"By old friends, I take it you are thinking of Marco Capitelli. Aamina?"

"Yes, Carlo, he was helpful, and need I say handsome and charming certainly helped?"

"My government, Aamina, is arranging to assemble the professional team to help as we speak, and Marco Capitelli is on top of the list."

"Carlo, does my smile betray me?"

"It does, Aamina; however, you can count on my discretion about—how should I say this—your warm feeling about working with Doctor Capitelli again."

Parma, Italy
Hotel Verdi

Standing on his balcony at Hotel Verdi, Marco Capitelli looked out on what promised to be a cloudy and possibly rainy day. Marco felt a strange unease. The balcony overlooked Parco Ducale, Parma's beautiful green oasis created for Napoleon's second wife, Maria Louise, when she resided in the city. The beauty of the park was enshrouded by dark shades invoked by the low-lying clouds. *Beauty and danger*, thought Marco. After another pensive moment, he reentered the bedroom and his eyes rested on the beautiful sleeping figure of Francesca Martini; beauty and danger, indeed, that a portrait of Giuseppe Verdi hung above the bed and the composer's watchful eyes rested upon Francesca confirmed his unease about their relationship.

Would his growing feelings for Francesca require him to like her native city of Parma? Parma, a city he often ridiculed vis-a-vis its competitive relationship with his beloved Bologna. Truth be known, his relationship with his absent father, who now resided within the region of Parma in the castled town of Compiano, shaded his view of this city. His father, although overtly warm and supportive of Marco's youthful ambitions, often seemed absent in Marco's life. Bologna, for him, held memories of his mother and her warm, supportive family. The fact that Compiano's castle seemed so imposing and physically menacing to young Marco's mind contributed to a sense of estrangement. His thoughts were interrupted when he sensed Francesca stirring.

"Marco, darling, get away from that window and bring that figure of David back to bed."

"Francesca—careful with your analogy of my body with that of Michelangelo's David. I might actually believe you."

"What do you mean, *might* believe me? You do believe it."

"I'll believe it if you acknowledge that in my eyes right now you remind me of a tempting Venus."

Lifting the bed sheet and revealing the lovely figure that would challenge Venus herself, Marco thought Botticelli gave Venus the scallop shell, but the bed sheets made the image even more tempting. Marco could not resist saying, "Francesca, it's time for breakfast, but suddenly my appetite lies right here in your arms."

Later
Breakfast at the Hotel

"So, Francesca, what would the esteemed maestro, Signore Verdi, recommend for breakfast for this simple Bologna boy?"

"Well, the cornetto con cream accompanied by espresso is tasty and sweet," she replied.

"Tasty and sweet, hmm, I thought I had that experience earlier this morning in our room," Marco said as a smile spread across his face.

"Well, am I here to enlighten you about Parma with a tour, or do you have some other sinister motive for visiting me?"

"If you take me through that enticing park that has captured my interest across from the maestro's hotel, I'll explain my sinister motives. By the way, your cornetto recommendation hit the mark. What will your dinner recommendation do to entice this Bologna boy?"

Francesca smiled.

Parco Ducale

The slow pace of the walk through the park captivated Marco's interest in Francesca's explanation of Maria Louise's French influence on the park. Her description of the city's design of wide boulevards, also with its distinct French design, made Parma unique.

"Tell me about her palace; did she have a hand in its design?" he asked, caught up in her enthusiasm and true love of her city.

"Actually, yes, but the palace has a strong influence from Austria since Maria drew on her early pre-Napoleonic years in Vienna."

"You know that this Bologna boy has not come to terms with the fact that the European Union chose her palace for the honor of Europe's center for the study of food and health?"

"Do you think you will ever be at peace with this, Marco?" she asked, not certain whether to laugh or touch his arm.

"We'll see how your dining recommendation helps seduce my resistance to your beautiful city. I see an imposing fortress ahead; what is its purpose, if I may ask?"

"That's the Palazzo Della Pilotta, and you are right to call it a fortress because it was a fort to protect Parma back in the day. Today, it is the home of the National Gallery and the Teatro Farnese."

"So, Francesca, we cross this bridge and enter your wonderful city."

"Are you game, Bologna boy?"

"Lead the way, temptress."

Moments Later

"It's an imposing river—except I have one question: why is the river without even a hint of water?"

"Well, there is a reasonable explanation for the lack of water; incidentally, the name of this river is the Parma River, a tributary of the Apennine mountains lake Santo. As such, the seasonally drying of the lake on it edges causes the Parma River to dry out seasonally as well."

"Wow, Francesca, you're a fountain of knowledge—but I should say, in this case, a fountain without water." He allowed himself a faint smile at his attempt at humor. "Proceed into your beautiful city."

Meandering through Parma, Francesca was unusually animated as she pointed out the unique octagonal baptistery with works of art created by Parmigianino. She searched Marco's eyes for any hint of awe, but alas, to no avail. Undeterred, she reminded him that the Teatro Regio, which she had arranged to give him a private tour, was the next and final step for any aspiring opera singer.

"How did this *teatro* win the reputation as the final step for opera singers before La Scala in Milano, Francesca?"

"Well, we know opera, Bologna boy, and as I have always maintained, which you still doubt, we know food as well. So, let me take you to my favorite restaurant a short walk from here; it's called Ristorante Parmigianino."

"Lead the way, Parma girl! By the way, why am I not surprised that you would take me to a restaurant named after your city's famous artist?"

Ristorante Parmigianino

While observing the friendly reception Francesca received from management and staff, Marco saw her in a new and pleasant light. Her relaxed demeanor gave no hint of the well-practiced, controlled professional regard Marco had received when they first met on a tarmac at da Vinci Airport.

"Why don't you order for me and impress me with your self-proclaimed superior Parma cuisine?"

"If you insist. For *la primo piatto*, try the brodo with shaved Parmigiano; of course, Reggiano mixed with our dried mushrooms from our Valmozzola region. A local Lambrusco wine will help to add to your culinary adventure."

After more pleasantries with the staff, she turned to him quizzically. "So," she asked, "why did you come here to see this Parma girl?"

He smiled at the directness of her question. "How should I start, Francesca? As you have demonstrated in our two previous professional encounters, you are an indispensable source of knowledge and a remarkably accomplished professional. It was in large part due to your contributions that we had a successful resolution of both daunting projects we worked on together." Marco paused to let this sink in, then continued. "I have been asked to be part of a team representing Italy that will work with the Ethiopians on an environmental project that will impact the entire region. I think your expertise is needed on the project, and I have given a request to our Italian Minister of International Economic Development Antonio Forte that you be part of the team; he's said yes to my request."

After a brief outline of Ethiopia's ambitious Renaissance Dam project and that country's request for Italian technological involvement, Marco explained the highly probable damage that could occur to a significant ancient church should an ancient riverbed be reactivated.

"So, are you asking me to help save any religious artifacts?" Francesca asked.

He looked at her and said, "Yes, your expertise and that of the Vatican in saving works of art has, by my intimate experience, a proven track record of success. I am looking at the one person whose involvement in this project would give it any hope of succeeding."

"I'm flattered by your use of the term *intimate experience*," a smiling Francesca said. "So, Bologna boy, I am intrigued. I'm sure I can join you and your team. Let's work out the time and logistics."

She paused, her serious demeanor giving way to a beatific smile. "But now, I want to recommend some Muscat a di Cremona to further inform your pallet of our superior cuisine."

Chinese Embassy
Addis Ababa, Ethiopia

Hu Lee was a man of many powerful traits well-suited for accomplishing China's global ambitions. Patience was not one of them; he did not suffer fools and delays, no matter how minor. He turned to his hand-picked team of equally ardent devotees to China's ambitions and charged them with the task of gathering those Ethiopians who, for lack of any other term, were indebted to China's financial largess.

"Remember, this dam is our avenue to economically and politically increase our influence in northwest Africa; failure is not an option."

Rome
The Vatican Library

Professor Thomas Magnani, tall and regal in his bearing, entered the windowless room and quickly surveyed its occupants. He was assigned to lead Italy's biggest engineering/construction venture untaken in Ethiopia since the 1935 ill-fated Italian invasion of the country. Everyone on his team was hand-picked by him except one, the Vatican's Francesca Martini.

Having acquiesced earlier to Marco Capitelli's insistence on her necessary inclusion in the project, he welcomed her with his legendary warm embrace.

"Doctor Martini, I know we all would benefit from hearing you explain the importance of the church's connection with Ethiopia. Please enlighten us."

"It would be my pleasure," Francesca replied. She walked to the front of the room, turned around, and addressed the gathering.

Francesca explained the connection went back to the fifteenth century with Ethiopian pilgrims arriving in Rome. And despite the 1935 invasion, Ethiopia's deep commitment to the Christian faith continued to exist even under current pressure from Islam and, more recently, from Chinese Marxist influence.

She concluded by saying, "We here in the Vatican have the experience and the wherewithal to protect religious works of art in the threatened churches by the proposed dam. The Coptic community has struggled to create and maintain these churches and we will try our best to ensure they survive. Always remember it's not for our glory but Ethiopia's."

Professor Magnani turned to Doctor Capitelli and, with a wry smile, said, "I see your faith in Doctor Martini is well founded."

Pointing to the neatly arranged piles of documents on the long marble table, Magnani instructed the team to take copies and absorb the contents. "Take a copy and be familiar with the material when we meet tomorrow."

Addis Ababa, Ethiopia
Chinese Embassy

Addressing his assembled team, Hu Lee stressed: "You must study their traits with an eye on their strengths and, more importantly, their weakness. One of their team members, Marco Capitelli, is part of the new Italian delegation because he was with the original group that worked on forging the reconciliation of Ethiopia and Italy after Italy's past intrusions into Ethiopia's sovereignty. We would like to tarnish his star. So, I asked one of our archeologists, a Chinese Marxist, Doctor Xin Chin, who resides in Rome, to offer his credentials to the Italians so he could accompany their team. His presence will help speed our attempt to discredit their efforts.

"I would like you to meet and support our newest member, Doctor of Archeological Architecture, Doctor Xin Chin. Doctor Chin, please stand up so everyone can see who you are."

The figure that rose from the chair and bowed to the audience was a tall, solidly built man dressed in a tailored tweed jacket that complimented his Italian outfit.

Hu Lee continued, "Doctor Chin, for our mission, has the added advantage of having been educated in Milan, Italy, and a friend and a fellow student in Milan with Doctor Francesca Martini, also a member of the Italian delegation. A reacquaintance with Doctor Martini could serve our intentions well." Hu Lee smirked as he added this last aside.

Rome
Antonio Forte's Office

Signor Forte addressed the Italian team gathered in his late baroque-period styled office. The large windows permitted rays of late afternoon light to illuminate the golden trim of his equally baroque desk, lending a mystique of power to Signor Forte's position.

The group included a natural Italian sensibility in the desire to combine art with practical skills. The Italians feel that any undertaking should commit to beauty. So, helping a former colony-now-ally achieve their national goal of a Renaissance Dam compels a great attempt on all the team to demonstrate this Italian gift to the world.

"I'll commence our introductions as soon as the last two of our assembly arrive." Signor Forte glanced at his watch just as Francesca and Marco entered the room.

"Ah, here they are. Does anyone here need an introduction to Signora Martini and Signor Capitelli?"

Before Signor Forte could continue, Xin Chin rose from his seat, approached Francesca, and exclaimed with a broad smile, "Francesca, what a pleasure to see you again. Seeing you brings back wonderful memories of my days with you in Milan."

Francesca concealed her feelings at the effusive recognition he gave her in front of all her professional colleagues. "Xin, you as well for me, what a pleasant surprise; let's spend some time getting caught up after the meeting."

Marco gave a slight hint of concern in the narrowing of his eyes as he perused Mr. Chin.

Da Vinci Airport

"We're all ready, I presume, for our adventure," Signor Forte said as he surveyed his hand-picked team. The team included Thomas Magnani, Aldo Manfredi, Francesca Martini, Marco Capitelli, and Xin Chin, whose inclusion in the group was largely due to his association with Francesca Martini.

When he was satisfied that everyone was there and he had their attention, he continued, "We'll be met by our Ethiopian counterparts at the Italian consulate in Addis Ababa, so familiarize yourselves with their dossiers during our journey.

"I believe Doctor Martini and Professor Capitelli are already familiar with Assefa Berhane, the Director of Ethiopian Antiquities, and Aamina Gebremichael, the Assistant Director of Ethiopian Antiquities. And of course, Carlo Monti, Italy's Ambassador to Ethiopia, will be there.

Francesca and Marco, I'm sure you'll be pleased to know Signor Berhane and Signor Monti have received well-deserved promotions since you last saw them two years ago.

"Oh, and one more thing I almost forgot to mention, Mr. Hu Lee, the Chinese Planning Commissioner for the dam project, will be joining us as an observer. He and his team have been involved with the project since the beginning."

Flight to Addis Ababa

"Professor Capitelli, I have a favor to ask of you," Xin Chin said. "I hope you don't mind my request to exchange seats with you so I can enjoy reacquainting myself with Doctor Martini. There is so much I want to share with her; my experiences in Italy have been exceptionally beneficial in no small measure due to the insights and, dare I say, confidence-building she imparted to me.'"

Marco was initially startled by the hovering presence of Chin. Marco thought about his response to this request: *I could say, 'Sure, make it brief. I want my seat back soon.' But no, that would be rude, and most likely, that answer would embarrass Francesca. Considering my first flight with her two years ago was less than successful, I might as well demonstrate a more nuanced and mature Marco.*

"Go right ahead, Professor Chin, please, be my guest. I'll sit in your seat for a while. I certainly understand the wonderful effect of knowing Doctor Martini." Marco gave Chin what he hoped appeared as a gracious smile and thought, *please don't make it too long.*

He struggled to make a less-than-effective show of indifference to their conversation. The little he heard could be provocative, and they laughed together.

Ethiopia
Addis Ababa International Airport

The flight was uneventful, except for a military jet escort they picked up upon reaching Ethiopia's border. The rebellion in the Tigray region reminded the Italians that Ethiopia had not had a period of peace for some time.

As they deplaned, Marco heard his and Francesca's names being called out with a hearty welcome by Carlo Monti, the newly appointed Italian ambassador.

Greetings and congratulations were exchanged among the group and after everyone was acknowledged and accounted for, the group piled into the Land Rovers waiting to take them to their hotel.

"My friends and new colleagues, please get settled in Addis Ababa's Grand Hotel. I know it's been a long day. Tomorrow we'll gather at the Ethiopian Ministry of Antiquities at 9:00 a.m.," Antonio Forte said as the hotel staff unloaded the luggage from the cars.

Ethiopian Ministry of Antiquities

The ministry was in a deco-era office constructed by the Italians during their ill-fated invasion circa the late 1930s. Mussolini required an Italian twist to the usual deco features. Specifically, an imposing ancient Roman grandeur designed to intimidate visitors. Francesca viewed this need for Mussolini's fascism as a reflection of deep-seated male insecurity.

They entered a vast windowless room, nondescript except for a long and huge marble table positioned directly under the flag of Ethiopia. Their footsteps echoed, giving the room a cavernous quality.

The Ethiopian delegation was already seated on one side of the table. When the group from Italy arrived, Director of Antiquities Assefa Berhane rose from his seat and motioned his Ethiopian team to follow suit.

Assefa smiled at the arriving group. "We welcome our Italian guests, some as old friends, some as new colleagues; thank you for joining us. We have arranged for your transportation to the site of the Renaissance Dam later this morning, where you will meet the representatives from China and the on-site team members.

"First, allow me to introduce you to our team. Today we will review the plans, progress, and logistics."

Assefa briefly introduced the group members, then said, "Please help yourselves to tea, coffee, and breakfast at the far end of the table."

Assefa approached Francesca and Marco, greeting them both with a warm embrace. They were delighted to see each other and the conversation was animated and descriptive, briefly recalling their initial encounter two years prior.

Talk quickly turned to the present and Francesca congratulated Assefa on her promotion, prompting a similar response by Marco.

"You are both so kind, and do I detect a closer friendship between Doctors Martini and Capitelli?"

"Assefa," Marco responded, "you always could detect any evasions on my part. Yes, we're friends." He looked briefly at Francesca. "Good friends," he added, "in no small measure due to your helpful guidance in our first adventure in your captivating country."

Now, smiling at the Italians, he said, "Let me introduce you to Doctor of

Archeology and Symbiology Zala Aaron. She has followed your careers closely." They were introduced to a slender woman with such a captivating smile that it could not hide a serious mind.

Zala Aaron held out her hand. "Let me just say I am looking forward to my time with your team. Please forgive my mangling of your beautiful Italian language." Her brown eyes lingered a fraction of a second too long on Marco.

Appearing not to notice, Francesca responded by saying, "We only wish we could speak your language, and to that point, I'll take this time to introduce you to our team member fluent in your language, Doctor Xin Chin, a specialist and friend of mine in architecture and archeology."

"We know of the doctor's reputation in Addis Ababa. He helped us restore this imposing edifice we stand in now."

Marco wondered why that little piece of information wasn't part of the Italians' dossier. Of course, the hasty way the team was assembled might account for it, and it left an uncomfortable feeling that perhaps they didn't know as much about Chin as they should.

Doctor Chin spoke briefly to Zala Aaron in their native language, then turned to his Italian team members, and quipped in Italian that Doctor Aaron's name translated meant *high mountain*. He said the high mountain was a fitting metaphor that accurately captures her intelligence and strength. Marco glanced over at Zala and saw she was blushing.

Addis Ababa Airport

An old, battered-looking military transport cargo plane waited for them at the airport. As they walked out on the tarmac, Assefa Berhane told them that the visit to the Renaissance Dam would be first. "Tomorrow we will travel to our second and final stop, the rock-honed church in Lalibela.

Remember that the church lies near Tigray and is, as you are aware, a militarily contested area where Tigray rebels are active. So, every precaution for your safety will be attended to. Now, let's get on board."

Renaissance Dam

Although the landing was somewhat uneventful, the weather was not so cooperative. Clouds of dust obscured the team's first impression of the admittedly half-completed dam.

The international team that greeted them were the already ensconced engineers. They consisted of Chinese, Sudanese, Egyptians, and former METEC engineers who had been carefully vetted and deemed trustworthy.

Doctor Zala Aaron took the initiative and made the formal introductions in complete command of the on-site operations.

"Let's tour the facilities and closely examine areas where your expertise can be applied. I'll explain what we have accomplished as we tour the premises. Of course, Doctor Chin, Professor Capitelli, Doctor Martini, Doctor Magnani, Doctor Manfredi, and I will be departing tomorrow for Lalibela to hopefully save our beautiful rock-honed church from any potential issues."

The team's inspection of the dam offered insights into why METEC had to be disbanded. Areas of concrete designed to offer significant structural support for the dam were corroding well before the completion of the project. A conspicuous trail of corruption and inefficiency plagued the project; suppliers of the concrete were paid in advance and in full, inspections were rare, and any reprimands were nonexistent. Often a blanket seal of approval by all business and government agencies was given. The project itself was shrouded in secrecy in terms of investigative reporting. There were murmurings within the group, but no one openly discussed it. It seemed to be the taciturn hope of the team that whatever egregious issues had transpired were due to the incompetence and corruption of METEC.

Turning to the assembled construction crew in front of them, Assefa Berhane broke the silence by telling her group, "We must not forget to thank our Chinese engineers and financial investors for continuing to work to complete this necessary endeavor for our region."

Turning to whisper to Marco, Francesca said, "I thought it was customary to thank those who perform a job well."

Lalibela Church of St. George

As they approached the highlands of Lalibela by air, Assefa gave the team a quick history of the significance of this region in Ethiopian lore.

"As you know, we will be addressing the probability of the church being damaged by the Renaissance Dam project if a now-dormant river beneath it were to be activated by the work being done."

She kept her historical explanation brief so the team could enjoy the spectacular view of the Lalibela church of St. George as the Ethiopian military helicopter descended onto the site.

From the air a large cross carved into the surface of the plateau was the only visible sign of the church. But the visible portion of the cross was remarkable in that it appeared in circumference to suggest the size of an American baseball field. And what was truly astonishing was that the church went down what would be the equivalent of five stories into solid bedrock and earth.

Assefa turned to Marco and said, "I'm sure you know that the first floor is the top of the church, so we are looking down into the church."

"Yes, Assefa, I knew that. But neither the photos nor the technical description of the structure do it justice; this is truly a national treasure. The question I have now is how will our team be lowered to the top of the first floor? The top of the first floor sounds illogical but true."

Assefa pointed to a band of men in dark-colored robes that lined the perimeter of the cross. "Do you see those Coptic priests?"

"Yes, I do."

"Well, we will land on top of the church, and they will lower us to an entrance door with something that looks like a large platformed pully system onto the lowest part of the church structure."

Marco sized up the area that she had pointed to. "What about the weight of the helicopter and everything on it?"

Assefa looked at him and could see the concern on his face. "That's a valid observation, Marco. And believe me, that contingency has been considered. In the bowels of this helicopter, we have a system that can do the job. It will calculate the level of safety as we proceed."

The landing required some intricate maneuvers that seemed second nature to the military pilots, no doubt due to Ethiopia's many years of internal and external wars.

Doctor Zala Aaron took the initiative and directed the crew toward the priests, motioning to where the copter should land. "Follow their instructions carefully. The lowering will be slow and appear uneven. Pay no attention if the platform should hit the side of the church and shake things up."

Francesca turned to Marco, saying, "Not quite reassuring, is she?" He was tempted to take Francesca's hand but thought it might not be the thing to do at the moment.

As forewarned, the descent into the first-floor portal was shaky and not without a few uncomfortable bumps alongside the rock-honed church of St. George. The entrance cut centuries ago accommodated people whose average height didn't anticipate the modern taller visitors.

Priests in flowing brown robes and strapped sandals offered assistance to steady the team taking their first steps into their religious domain.

When they finally reached the base of the structure, Zala Aaron requested the team take off their shoes and observe the quiet of the priests.

No matter how many times Francesca had seen photos of the beautiful religious mosaics painted on the church walls and columns, the sheer size and vibrancy of the colors stunned her. Her preview and therefore primary knowledge was of Western art offered by the Vatican, where she worked. Now, in this obsessively primitive setting, her prejudices were challenged by the obvious religious fervor that produced these images of the Coptic faith seen through Ethiopian eyes.

"I feel profoundly humble amid these stunning representations of our mutual faith," she whispered to Marco.

"You're not alone, Francesca. I'm amazed at the many references to our lady and baby Jesus. Members of Ethiopia's royal linage always accompany them, with King Lalibela prominently displayed. It's remarkable."

The priests, as if in unison, pointed to a descending stairwell. Zala reminded them that silence was not only requested but mandatory when approaching each new room of the church.

"We can assemble and begin to perform our assigned tasks when we reach the last level or the bottom floor. Then we will receive the blessing of our hosts."

Upon arriving at the lowest level, Assefa Berhane thanked the priests for their blessings.

She turned to his assembled team and said, "We can begin our task now. I will ask you to state your specific role in this project, beginning with Doctor Chin."

Chin gave a slight nod of acknowledgment to Assefa and briefly told the group he would be applying his archeological and Chinese language skills to facilitate communications and that he would also serve as an interpreter for Mr. Hu Lee, head of the Chinese delegation.

Doctor Magnani followed and said he would be addressing geological issues. Aldo Manfredi stated he would be focused on engineering issues. Professor Capitelli, to keep his role description brief, said he would address any archeological anomalies that appear during the project. Finally, Doctor Martini said she would focus on preserving the beautiful and historical religious art.

With his customary sense of expediency, Doctor Magnani motioned the team to look at a cavity indentation parallel to the ground floor–side of the church. Pointing out specific areas of the rock bed darker in color than the rest, Magnani claimed the cavity was a dormant riverbed.

Magnani consulted his computer before continuing. After nodding his head as if in affirmation of what he saw on the computer, he said to the group, "Our satellite imagery seems to confirm that this cavity indentation aligns with the dormant riverbed. The same riverbed that we are certain will be reactivated by the Renaissance Dam."

For the first time since they arrived at the site, Hu Lee spoke. "Before we accept your perspective, Doctor Magnani, I would like to confirm your findings with our satellite imaging sources. Please don't take any offense with this, but it is well known that our Chinese satellites contain technology that, quite frankly, Italy doesn't possess."

"No offense taken," was Doctor Magnani's reply.

"I don't know about you, Marco, but I'm a bit offended; what say you?" Francesca whispered as an aside.

"You can count me as an offended member, Francesca."

"I couldn't help overhearing you and Francesca." Doctor Xin Chin, leaning in, whispered too.
"Let's see first how this plays out. You know Chinese can make mistakes too, as I did by not staying in touch with you, Francesca."

"I'm flattered, Xin. Meanwhile, I want to examine that interesting mural on the ceiling to my right."

Marco was surprised at his visceral reaction to the last part of Chin's remarks. He stayed quiet and tried to show a neutral expression, but his placid demeanor couldn't dissuade Francesca from observing his slight discomfort.

Upon closer examination Francesca saw that the mural was a representation of Enoch, the great-grandfather of Noah. Marco had joined her in front of the mural shortly after the exchange between them and Chin, and soon, the team was in front of the mural. Francesca and Marco began to tell the other team members about the significance of Enoch in Ethiopian religious lore, and Assefa Berhane enthusiastically joined the dialogue.

"Enoch is given a place of honor in our culture. Our Jewish heritage predates our Christian heritage. He is usually shown as a figure hovering above the earth and looking down on God's creation. According to the Bible, the angels tell him to his left in this mural that God will destroy his creation for their disobedience. Further, when cast back to Earth, Enoch lands here in Ethiopia. Ultimately Noah, his great-grandson, saves a remnant of God's creation from the flood."

"Assefa, neither Marco nor I could have explained this as well, and certainly not with your passion. The question now is, can this and other paintings be saved?"

Doctor Aldo Manfredi, who had been listening, called the team's attention to cracks above the Enoch mural. He saw that the pressure of a reunited riverbed would cause additional stress that would damage the mural and weaken the stone columns that supported the floors above.

Marco and Doctor Magnani concurred, pointing to additional cracks near the stairwell and, more importantly, adjacent to the dried riverbed.

Doctor Manfredi turned to his Chinese counterparts, Hu Lee and Xin Chin. "I would like to have an analysis done by our engineering department in Rome that would show the effect of the Renaissance Dam's projected volume of water as it relates to the ability of the Lalibela church to withstand the pressure. So, Signor Lee, could you please have your officials at the Dam forward the requested information to Rome with a copy sent to me?"

Later

Privately, Hu Lee addressed Xin Chin.

"Now it is our duty to the party to thwart this Italian effort involving this church. Our man at the Dam will create an analysis to dispute their analysis. Then you, Chin, will raise doubts in the minds of the Ethiopian representatives, particularly Assefa Berhane. Also, use your friendship with Francesca Martini to place some seeds of doubt and dissension between her and Doctor Capitelli, especially as it relates to his analysis."

Xin Chin spoke with Zala Aaron.

"Do I have your assurance, Doctor Aaron, that Assefa Berhane is unaware of the true circumstances surrounding the death of the Renaissance Dam chief engineer?"

"As I have said repeatedly, she is in the dark, but it is up to you to ensure that she remains so. Your concern should be Doctor Capitelli, as he, no doubt, will make a compelling case to protect this church. He will enlist the help of Doctor Martini, and I am sure she will corroborate his findings. So, Chin, you would be well advised to use your charm to dissuade her cooperation with Capitelli. As far as the chief engineer's demise, it is best that you do not question the circumstances of his death. To that end, Hu Lee and I have deliberately kept you in the dark."

My charm, Chin thought, *is a meager product to rely on.* The only thing he knew for certain was his friendship with Francesca was something he would not so easily wish to lose.

Church of St. George

Francesca, cramped beneath the Coptic murals, heard footsteps approaching from behind. Assuming it was Marco, she called out to him, "Marco, come and see this intriguing anomaly of Enoch."

"Francesca, do my footsteps sound like Marco?"

Turning her head, she smiled as Xin slowly came into focus.

"Xin, I should know how to distinguish between you by now. To what do I owe this welcomed intrusion to my work?"

"Glad it is welcomed. I wanted to hear your take on the perceived water issues and if they are threats to these works of art."

Francesca looked at Xin for a moment before answering. "Well, If the riverbed rises to a level our engineers foresee, then It looks like old Enoch himself could suffer cracks along his face and chest and a significant diminishing of the well-preserved colors that have survived for centuries in this air-tight environ."

"Francesca, Enoch—if my religious memory back in Milan serves me—lived hundreds of years. Maybe a couple of cracks might look more realistic for him."

"Xin, I expect that kind of humor from Marco—but not from my serious student friend back in Milan."

Xin winced. Francesca wasn't certain whether it was from her mild reprimand or her reference to Marco. "Marco again," replied Xin. "I can't seem to escape him. Incidentally, where is the dear boy?"

Francesca responded, "I heard that he is in communication with Egyptian archeologists he knows. Apparently, the lessons learned in the 1960s construction of the Aswan Dam might aid our assessment of this project."

Marco relayed his conversation with the Egyptians to Assefa Berhane.

"Marco, my friend, why the forlorn expression?"

Not knowing how to express his confusion with the information his Egyptian counterparts conveyed, Marco asked Assefa to listen to his phone conversation and lend her thoughts.

"Of course, I'll be glad to lend a hand—or should I say, ear, Marco."

Moments Later

"Marco, I think I have an obligation to convey this conversation to the Director of Ethiopian Antiquities, Aamina Gebremichael."

Marco replied, "Assefa, if you think it is appropriate for me to give my insights on this matter to the director, I'd be glad to."

Marco highlighted the Egyptian engineer's confusion with earlier texts and emails with the Renaissance Dam Chief Engineer Biruk Arega. The Egyptians claimed that Arega expressed concern with unsubstantiated reports of progress in meeting the Dam's completion date. Specifically, the information concerning the effect on the dormant riverbed was unclear. The Egyptians recalled the damage that the building of the Aswan Dam in the 1960s did to temples and the Soviet Union overseer's reluctance to address these concerns for fear of Moscow's loss of prestige.

"It seems, Assefa," Marco stressed, "that at that time, the American engineers' working on preserving temples from damage by the future Lake Nasser forced a reluctant acquiescence by the Soviet engineers."

Later

Assefa recapped all of Marco's concerns for Director Gebremichael. As Assefa's discussion with the director continued, they both agreed that in addition to addressing Marco's concerns, they should also ask the Egyptian government to send them copies of the transcripts of their correspondence with Chief Engineer Arega.

Hours Later
Office of the Director of Ethiopian Antiquities

A worried expression defiled her normal smooth and inviting facial continence. Director Gebremichael, upon hearing of the Egyptian correspondence with Chief Engineer Arega, shouted to her staff to arrange an immediate flight to the Renaissance Dam.

Mr. Hu Lee's Office
The Renaissance Dam

Lee's face, normally void of any discernable expression, revealed a deep concern. He rose quickly from his desk and shouted to his subordinates: "Get Xin Chin here immediately!"

Xin Chin received Lee's text while discerning a curious anomaly concerning Enoch's expression. Francesca shared his perplexed expression. As students back in Milan, they often recognized similar insights in their exploration of religious art. Their latest project brought back ease in how they related to each other.

"What do you make of this, Xin?" she asked. Before he could reply, she said, "I think Enoch has a worried expression as he gazes down from his lofty heavenly position."

"Francesca, the Ethiopians would probably claim that his gaze is a worried and loving concern for their country. Considering that this painting was commissioned in the fourteenth century during the reign of King Lalibela, it would mean that Ethiopia was under siege by a hostile Islam at that time." Before continuing his mural analysis, he received a text, which he read immediately. "I'm so sorry. I seem to be required to leave you and make a quick appearance back at the Renaissance Dam. There is a helicopter waiting for me on the church's roof."

Francesca thought that using a church's roof would seem odd, at best, but with these churches cut into the ground rather than built up from the ground, it was not so unusual.

"Xin, when you get back, we can pick this up and explore this further. In the meantime, I'll get Marco's take on this."

"Marco again! How do I diminish him in your mind?" He smiled at her. "A daunting task."

"I'm afraid, Xin, you have your work cut out for you. But I'm flattered you're trying."

Two Hours Later

Xin approached Lee's office, illuminated with large strobe lights pointing at his desk through a long and dark cavernous hallway. Lee appeared pensive and somewhat nervous. Xin intuitively slowed his approach. Years of dealing with superiors in China's command society conditioned subordinates to be prepared with answers to please. Xin set his confident facial expression, perfected over the years, and walked into Lee's office.

Hu Lee placed his finger on text transcripts and commanded Xin to read them out loud.

Xin noticed Lee's concern and intuitively knew Lee would expect Xin to facially express an equal concern.

Xin read the contents quickly to himself before commenting. "Your concern is valid, comrade," replied Xin. He read the text out loud.

Destroy, by any means, the hard copy that Assefa Berhane receives from her Egyptian counterparts. I have already alerted our comrades in Egypt to remove corroborating information at that end. Zala Aaron will aid our task by using her prestige and influence to distract the Ethiopian authorities.

After reading the text, he looked at Lee, who said, "Remember, Xin, Zala gained the friendship of Ethiopia's Chief Engineer Biruk Arega." Lee smiled ruefully to himself, remembering how she had made the engineer's death look like a suicide. Returning to his conversation with Xin, he said, "She is very resourceful."

Lee had to suppress another smile, realizing Xin's unawareness of Zala Aaron's ruthlessness.

"Now, go perform your duty for your country."

Lalibela Church

The helicopter from Egypt made a slow descent toward the church's roof, unable to avoid the raising of century-old dust and debris. A team of Egyptian officials, covering their faces from the debris, exited the aircraft.

Assefa Berhane identified herself as the recipient of their written documents.

"As you can see, we are reluctant, in this religious setting, to hold a governmental meeting in this church. So, if you are amenable, we can discuss this matter on the roof. I can assure you the weather will cooperate. After we talk briefly amongst ourselves, I'll have my colleagues Francesca Martini, Marco Capitelli, and Xin Chin join us."

Later

"These transcripts are clear to me," Assefa said with a worried expression. "I already reported this back to Director Gebremichael. Geologist Magnani and engineer Manfredi have already been informed back at the Renaissance Dam. Now that you have read them, do you share my concern?"

Nodding in unison, Marco and Francesca agreed. Xin Chin, however, said he would question further the Egyptian assertion by the late Biruk Arega that corruption was involved.

"Xin, I appreciate your caution, but I have no time to waste," said Assefa. "Even if you are correct, an investigation must be undertaken now. Remember, METEC was abandoned because of corruption."

"Assefa, please understand I want my language skills to corroborate some Chinese correspondence to support these allegations. If you can allow me to examine these documents against some of my sources, I'm sure your position will be further strengthened."

"Xin, as usual, you're making a compelling case. Okay, take some time, but not too much, and examine these documents."

Xin wondered how to accomplish the task of destroying this document without appearing to have had a hand in it. He wondered how many copies existed and who else may have had access to the documents. As he descended toward the bowels of the church, he received a text from one of the Egyptians who delivered the original document by helicopter: *My name is Lieutenant Khan. I'm here to help you with your task. I'll meet you by the riverbed beneath the Enoch painting.* Xin found this message cryptic but demanding; there was no choice but to follow the request. He thought for a moment and realized it wasn't a request but a command.

Xin reached the location before Khan and waited under the mural for Khan to arrive. Moments later, under the stern gaze of Enoch, a man dressed as a pilot in Egyptian military garb appeared.

"I'm sure you can appreciate the irony in our meeting place, Doctor Chin. We destroy their proof while their nations' protectors watch helplessly." It seemed to Xin that Khan enjoyed this.

Xin, feigning a smile, found the Egyptian's remark difficult to accept. Destroying the document was one thing. But destroying this Ethiopian symbol of their nation challenged his sense of patrimony and professional vocation. Preserving and restoring art was at the core of his being.

"Tell me, how do you intend to do this?" Xin inquired.

The Egyptian, still gazing up at the painting of Enoch but now using his finger, pointed toward cracks beneath the biblical figure's face.

"It seems there is an untraceable chemical applicant that I will place near this crack that will cause the painting to collapse once the piece is ignited. If, by chance, the document in question were to be carelessly dropped moments before this destructive chemical does its duty, who is to question such an unfortunate accident?"

Accident, Xin thought, *just like the "suicide" of Biruk Arega?*

"You don't think we can pull this off?" asked Khan, staring at the man in front of him and with whom he would need to cooperate for the plan to work.

Xin quickly changed his facial expression to sublime confidence and added words to back up his expression. "Assefa Berhane, Ethiopia's Director of Antiquities, is the only one holding this document and she must deliver it to his superiors after her investigation of its allegations is completed. So, how do we hope she will drop the document when we ignite the destruction of old Enoch?"

The lieutenant's response was accompanied by a cold smile. "You, Mr. Chin, will lead Berhane to this spot and ask her to elaborate on her findings. I will remain unseen but nearby. Excuse yourself for a moment. I'll leave timing up to you, and I'll ignite the chemical. Think of it this way: we destroy the evidence along with the only person who could corroborate the document. Hu Lee has great faith in you and me as an Egyptian in his payroll, wishing to continue in his enriching friendship."

Smiling, Khan acknowledged that the lieutenant's order from Lee would—to be more precise—assure that Xin and Assefa would die in the tragic accident. Two birds, one stone, no witnesses.

Moments later, on a higher church floor, Assefa received Xin's text, asking her to meet him by the dried riverbed beneath Enoch's portrait.

"You must excuse me, Marco. Your rival for Signora Francesca's affection summons me."

"Assefa, where would you get such an idea?"

"You must know that even though I'm getting older, I can still read intentions. Especially when it comes to the affairs of the heart."

"Assefa, I hope you're in my corner; you're too formidable not to be."

"Marco, have faith that I am."

Minutes Later
Beneath Enoch's Portrait

Xin Chin welcomed Assefa with an uncustomary hug. Glancing at the document in his hand, he asked if any new allegations could be leveled at the so-called suicide of Chief Engineer Biruk Arega.

Assefa, rather than answering his question, extended the document toward Chin.

"Here, look for yourself. It appears that Chief Engineer Biruk Arega saw all statistical observations concerning a reactivated river and knew it would undermine the stability of this church. The Egyptian document highlights the damage to the art of Ethiopian religious icons in the church." Looking over her shoulder toward Enoch with a sad smile she added, "The chief engineer must have felt a rush of Ethiopian patriotism. It is clear in the final message he sent. That begs the question of why he would commit suicide after he sent the message."

Xin's expression of concern was accompanied by a glance over his shoulder, where he saw Lieutenant Khan hidden in the shadows of a darkened religious column, pointing a gun at Assefa.

"Assefa Berhane, you are to keep the document; after all, you are an Ethiopian patriot. What an honor to die for your country. Does it surprise you that Doctor Chin would also be a patriot for his country?"

Khan emerged from the shadows with his gun still pointed at Assefa.

Looking with undisguised anger at Xin, Assefa implored, "Would you seek profit at the expense of your country?"

"I hate to interrupt this sentimental conversation, but I need to ask you to stand directly beneath your national protector. You should know the manner of your death. As Doctor Chin knows full well, we have a chemical implant beneath old Enoch. It seems we can add some new wrinkles to his aged continence. Xin, I need you to join Doctor Berhane under the portrait of Enoch."

Xin lunged at Khan with a warrior's cry. The sudden movement and the loud cry momentarily surprised Khan, who wasn't anticipating any resistance. Khan quickly recovered and viciously smashed his handgun against Xin's temple.

"Well, your newfound sense of right and wrong is a surprise. But we should have sensed your time in the decadent West, particularly with Signora Martini and her Vatican religious illusions, would have its effect. Why don't you move alongside Doctor Berhane so when old Enoch comes tumbling down, he can take both of you with him? You know, Xin, we intended to dispense with you later—this seems more efficient, don't you think?"

As he reached for the ignition device to set off the explosion, Khan felt his gun grabbed—by Marco. Unable to wrestle it free from Khan, Marco was pushed against Enoch's mural and forced to lie next to Xin and Assefa.

"I heard your cry, Xin! But as you can see, I'm out of my league. Assefa, I'm so sorry."

"We still have a weapon!" Xin whispered urgently to Marco.

"Draw his attention to me quickly when he lowers his head." Chin glanced at Marco's leg and smiled.

Assefa, mustering as much confidence as she could, said, "Khan, you think you will leave here intact? The priests will never let you leave. Their sole mission is to revere and protect Enoch."

"Tell me, Berhane." Khan leaned in to underscore his point. "Do you actually believe that Hu Lee and I didn't anticipate this?"

Suddenly Marco jumped up. He delivered a ferocious kick to Khan's head that rendered Khan unconscious. His gun fell from his hand and the chemical ignition dropped to the floor. Marco quickly picked up both items.

Assefa and Chin stood up and joined Marco in shouting for help.

48 Hours Later
Outside the Prime Minister's Office
Addis Ababa

Visibly anxious, Francesca said, "I can't hear what's transpiring—but Assefa Berhane and Director Aamina Gebremichael have been in there over an hour."

"The suspense is unnerving, to say the least, Francesca. By the way, Marco," Xin intoned, "That was some kick you administered to Lieutenant Khan. I venture to guess that your experience on the soccer field had something to do with this. Francesca told me what a powerful asset you were to your team because of your kicking skills. I must say, your demonstration was impressive."

"I wasn't a first-string player, for sure, and I don't even recall many successful overhead shots in my less-than-stellar university career. All I knew was that Khan's head was perfectly aligned and my leg sprung into motion."

"Three cheers for that leg of yours, Marco!"

At that moment, the prime minister's security guards opened his office door. They motioned Francesco, Marco, and Xin to enter.

Standing next to the prime minister, the smiling expressions of Doctor Berhane and Doctor Gebremichael succeeded in calming any reservation's group may have had.

"Please receive my hand in sincere gratitude for your selfless service to my country," the prime minister enthused. "Allow me to tell you what has transpired in the last few days. Hu Lee and Doctor Zala Aaron have been arrested. The confession of Lieutenant Khan, to use an American expression, spilled the beans. No doubt, this confession was ably assisted by a rather well-timed hit to his head by Doctor Capitelli. Chief engineer Biruk Arega did not commit suicide; Doctor Aaron poisoned him. He, of course, had a long-term professional relationship with the doctor and would have been very trusting of her presence in his isolated office at the Renaissance Dam."

As these sad revelations sank in with his audience, the prime minister continued. "As the expression goes, always follow the money. In this case, China, our largest source of funds to build this dam, wished to cover any misappropriations of money METEC received. Doctor Aaron has admitted as much and hasn't exhibited much remorse. She will probably have a lot of time in jail to reflect on her decisions. The Chinese government has asked for the extradition of Mr. Lee. I'm sure he won't have a warm reception. Now I come to the question of Mr. Xin Chin—what to do?"

Calling Chin into a private conversation, which seemed to last an eternity, the prime minister finally motioned Francesca and Marco to join them.

"I want to state this declaration of forgiveness toward Doctor Chin. Agreeing with my compatriots Doctor Berhane and Doctor Gebremichael, Doctor Chin acted not as an agent of Mr. Lee but a respecter of Ethiopian heritage."

A visible expression of relief and humility covered Xin's face. Francesca rushed to him and enveloped him in her arms.

Later
Italian Embassy

"Marco, Xin asked me to see him when we return to Rome. It seems that my influence with the government and the Vatican will expedite his return to their good graces. I wanted you to hear this first from me."

Marco hesitated in gathering his next words. "Francesca, I can see his desire for you, and I must admit that he has many outstanding qualities." Marco hesitated, then resumed speaking. "He is a good man, and if you love him, then I wish you both a world of happiness. If you choose him over me, it will hurt. But his love for you is real.

"I'll leave for Rome on another flight with geologist Magnani and engineer Manfredi. Whatever your decision, perhaps we can enjoy a tradition one more time that has become important to me and meet for dinner at the rooftop Eton Hotel? Just let me down gently if he wins your heart. Oh, and one more thing: the invitation for the rooftop extends to him if it is your wish. If he comes with you, I will have my answer regarding our future."

A Few Days Later
Rooftop of Eden Hotel

Rome's panorama didn't disappoint Marco. The usual seductive light tinge of red embraced the skyline of the city's famous icons. Now, if only he could share this romantic setting with Francesca and not his rival in love, Xin.

A text from Francesca proclaimed her imminent arrival. Marco felt an uncharacteristic lack of confidence. A confidence honed over the years with his customary belief that women were always attracted to him. Francesca was the awakening in his self-awareness that women—to truly feel attractive—need to be convinced of the man's understanding of the woman's unique value.

The waiter tapped Marco on the shoulder, announcing the arrival of his guest, Doctor Martini. Marco turned quickly, rising from his chair, and smiled. His eyes darted beyond her to see if Xin was with her. He couldn't bring himself to ask her if Xin was coming; he wasn't sure he wanted to hear the answer.

Francesca sat down softly and, as if she knew his thoughts, said, "No, Marco. Xin will not be coming tonight."

"Are you with me tonight so I can have my last memory of you alone before your exit with Xin?"

"Marco, if I'm going to make an exit, it is with you—for life. What's holding back that loquacious young man I thought I knew so well?"

"Francesca, are you choosing me? Before you answer that, please accept this Baci chocolate and read what it says inside." He accompanied the request by kneeling on his knee.

Francesca opened the box of candy, expecting to read the chocolate's usual romantic saying. But this time, a small handwritten scrap of paper with illegible writing had replaced the usual romantic sayings that appear with all the candies. She squinted in the light, trying to read the message. "I think it says: 'Will you marry me?'"

Raising her head with a loving smile, she exclaimed, "Yes, Bologna boy! Yes, yes, if only to cure you of your evil ways. If I seemed hesitant in the past, it is because I wanted to see what your mentor, Italy's famous archeologist Count Farnese, saw in you. Marco, you have the qualities he saw, and now I see them. You selflessly recognized Xin's decent qualities. You would not diminish them in my eyes, even if it meant you would lose me. So, I'm yours, and I love you. Marco. And I know you are going to love living in Parma."

Oh, God. Parma, Marco thought. *Did I make a mistake?*

The End, Perhaps…

Postscript

Conversation in another corner of the world

"Well, you heard my proposal. Doctor Capitelli could be the instrument that will restore our heritage. Any thoughts or objections?"

"Well, the obvious one is how can we persuade the doctor to undertake this task and yet deny him the truth of our goal?"

"Leave that up to the interested parties and me. The doctor seeks projects of historical enlightenment. We believe we can make a compelling case that he will find hard to refuse. Keeping the Italian government in the dark might be easier if they allow Doctor Capitelli to work with our own archeologists. Remember, our sources confirm the Italian government's deep trust in Signore Capitelli."

"If the Italians do find out, what then?"

"Let's just say, using an American expression, 'We'll make them an offer they can't refuse.'"

Author Comments on the Actual History

Regarding the first story, *The Obelisk*:

An Obelisk was taken from Axium, Ethiopia in 1935 and kept as a war trophy in Rome for 70 years.

An early invasion of Ethiopia by Italy resulted in an Italian defeat in 1889.

Regarding the second story, *The Silver Altar*:

Charlemagne did endow the original Saint Peter's basilica with a silver altar in the year 811. Muslim raiders in 848 raided Saint Peter's, and absconded with the Silver Altar. Its whereabouts is still unknown.

Parts of modern-day southern Sudan were Christian before succumbing to Islam during this period.

President Jefferson did create the first American Navy, which sent our forces to the Islamic world of North Africa in the eatly1800s to free captive American sailors.

Boko Haram does operate in North Africa as a terrorist organization.

Regarding the third story, *The Blue Nile Blues*:

METEC, as an Ethiopian metal and engineering enterprise, was recently disbanded because of corruption.

On a personal note: My father, Thomas A. Rossi, was born and raised in the United States. As a young man of 20, he visited his Italian parents in Italy in 1935. Motivated by revenge for the 1889 defeat, Mussolini was seeking to raise an army for the 1935 Italian invasion of Ethiopia. Knowing that the Italian government would seek to draft him in spite of his American citizenship, my father left Italy and returned to the United States. He would later marry my mother and serve in the US Army during WWII.

For me, Ethiopia looms large in my mind since I wondered what would have happened to him had he participated in that unlawful invasion.

Acknowledgments

I'd like to thank, first and foremost, my wife Patricia for her constant support and encouragement to write my story.

Additionally, I thank Naomi Rosenblatt, my publisher, whose insights and guidance lent confidence to my natural insecurity whenever I doubted its completion. Naomi (Noni) is responsible for the lovely drawings that highlight this story.

A thank you to my niece, Ellen Blair, for her early encouraging comments about my writing style. She has demonstrated, in her own career, a unique ability to review books of various authors.

To my cousin Peter who helped create images and ideas for Marco's adventures.

To my friend, John Mercogliano, for giving me the title *The Silver Altar*.

To all my friends and relatives who encouraged me throughout the process.

And in memory of Josie Corti, who was one of my first readers.

About the Author

ROBERT ROSSI is a life-long resident of Manhattan's Midtown East Side, raised with an awareness of his Italian ancestry. His grandparents emigrated to America from Parma, imparting a sense of wonder about Italian historical experience. This work is a homage to the Capitelli (his mother's maiden name) and Rossi (his father's name) sides of the family.

www.ingramcontent.com/pod-product-compliance
Lightning Source LLC
Chambersburg PA
CBHW040017250626
47171CB00006B/35